SONG
OF THE
RED
SQUIRE

SONG OF THE
RED
SQUIRE

C.W. BLACKWELL

NOSETOUCH PRESS

CHICAGO | PITTSBURGH

Song of the Red Squire

Copyright © 2022 by C.W. Blackwell
All Rights Reserved.

ISBN-13: 978-1-944286-26-2
Paperback Edition

Published by Nosetouch Press
www.nosetouchpress.com

For more information, contact Nosetouch Press:
info@nosetouchpress.com

Cataloging-in-Publication Data

Names: Blackwell, C.W., author.
Title: Song of the Red Squire
Description: Chicago, IL : Nosetouch Press [2022]
Identifiers: ISBN: 9781944286262 (paperback)
Subjects: LCSH: Horror—Fiction. | Paranormal—Fiction.
GSAFD: Horror fiction. | BISAC: FICTION / Horror.

Cover & Interior designed by Christine M. Scott.
www.clevercrow.com

Tree leaf art by Rustic @AdobeStock.

FOR THOSE WHO WANDER
THE HIGH COUNTRY ROADS
AND RUTTY TWO-TRACKS,
OUT WHERE THE FIR AND SPRUCE
TREES GROW, WHERE MOSS LEATHERS
THE OLD STONE MARKERS ON
SPURRED AND HAWK-SHADOWED
TRAILS: WHEN YOU HEAR A SONG
COME RISING FROM THOSE
LONELY COVES AND HOLLOWS,
THROUGH THE HELLS
OF HOLLY AND ROSEBAY—
LISTEN, LISTEN, AND TAKE HEED.

———————————

PART ONE

*The raven spread
her wings o'black*

*The jack leapt
from the briar*

*The buck did raise
his thorny rack*

*And bit that
ol' Red Squire*

**—WYLDTON
NURSERY
RHYME**

THE PASSENGER TRAIN RUMBLED

through foothills and hickory groves under a dirty cloud of smoke, passing small towns and nameless shanties alike. Charlie Danwitter watched the countryside pass before him with mute curiosity: a tobacco farm sweeping down a hillside, a wooden trestle over rust-colored water. Figures bent crooked amid their daily labors with pack mules and crated animals at their feet. He marveled how he'd once crossed the Atlantic, chased the German army across the Belgian line—but he'd never ventured west of Greensboro, North Carolina.

The hickory gave way to maple, and soon those thinned, too. Coming into West Jefferson, it appeared all the trees had been clear-cut straight back to the slopes of the Blue Ridge Mountains. The land now lay stubbled with the corpse of a hardwood forest, and over that corpse roamed a multitude of pigs and chickens and men. He spotted a caravan of timber trucks coming down the mountain about a mile off, loaded with whatever they could still find up there.

How far the forest would recede was anyone's guess. All the way to the Tennessee line, he imagined.

He sorted his things, checked the luggage claim ticket in his breast pocket. He could feel the great pistons beneath him slowing as the train neared the station. It was still early, morning fog curling back over the mountain peaks. Behind the ridgeline, fog pooled like water against a dam. It whitened the sky all the way to the horizon.

He looked closer—something stirred there.

Some kind of disturbance wallowed in the weather.

From the sea of fog rose a strange ethereal figure. A wraithlike face with moon eyes and a great void mouth. The head twisted and bore its nightmare eyes on the train. It seemed fixed on Charlie's window as it crested the summit and came wending into the valley, white tendrils casting about like spiders' legs.

He pulled a glass vial from his coat pocket and tapped a single pill into the well of his palm, popped it into his mouth, and swallowed it dry. He shut his eyes tightly. Knuckles white over the wooden lip of the armrest.

Just close your eyes and breathe.

He heard conversations starting up around him as sleepers woke and prepared to disembark. A pair of old men played chess across the aisle, and one had just put the other in check. A woman grumbled to herself about the meal service. A teenage boy was complaining how much he missed home. Charlie heard the vestibule doors open, the sound of a meal cart squeaking down the aisle. He opened his eyes and held up a finger and the attendant came to him.

"Is it too late for a glass of water?" Charlie asked.

The attendant looked him over with alarm.

"You don't look so good, sir."

"I'm just thirsty is all."

"Train-sick maybe. Let me see what I can find." He dug through the bottom shelf of the cart and produced a sweaty half-gallon jug of cider. "This is all I have."

Charlie acquiesced with a quick nod. The attendant poured the cider into a glass mug and handed it to him.

"You can open that window if it makes you feel better," said the attendant.

"I'd rather not."

"It's a pleasant morning. The air might help."

"There's no need. We're almost there."

"Suit yourself. Just don't get sick on me. Made it all the way from Abingdon without nobody gettin' sick."

"I'll be fine," said Charlie. "Just a little spell. What do I owe you?"

"Keep your stomach in one piece and we're even."

Charlie drank the cider and pressed the cold glass to his forehead. Sweat gathered at his temples. When he caught his breath, he glanced out the window. He saw nothing strange about the town. A bank with a large brick wall and white painted letters came into view. A row of clapboard houses angled up the hill. He counted two general stores. Above the town, mountain slopes flooded with sunlight. Red maples ablaze in the high draws. The fog had receded, and it left behind a few ragged clouds adrift in the valley, slowly dissolving.

At the West Jefferson depot, he wandered through a small crowd with a wool coat draped over one arm and a travel bag shouldered over the other. The air was cool and smelled of chimney smoke and rail grease. He waited at the baggage claim with a dozen other passengers until the porter arrived with the luggage. When it was his turn at the counter, he claimed a duffel and a large tan suitcase and asked where he could find the car rental kiosk.

"Brand new building at the south end of the depot," said the porter. He looked down at Charlie over the top of his eyeglasses. "Just keep walking till you see all those pretty Fords."

He thanked him and laid a quarter on the counter, then gathered his suitcase and headed that way alongside the great black locomotive as it belched and steamed on its crankpins.

He tipped his hat at the engineer and the man offered a nod from the dark of his window. At the end of the gangplank was a short stairwell that emptied into a parking lot. There were six cars lined up beside a small kiosk. A mix of '47s and '48s. Blue, black, and red sedans.

"Mr. Danwitter?" A fat man squeezed out of the kiosk with a clipboard in his hand and a pencil behind his ear. He wore a tight-fitting shirt and a vest that buckled under the buttons. Sweat stains darkened his pits. "Are you Charles Danwitter?"

"One and the same." Charlie set down his suitcase and shook his hand. "I think I'm supposed to talk to you about a car."

"Indeed you are. I'm Larry Hedsel. Your employer called ahead and arranged everything. But I got to correct you on one small point."

"Did I say something wrong already? Seems like I just got here."

Hedsel was blushing and looking over the row of rental cars.

"Well, it's just that they—we—thought a truck might be more appropriate for the kind of travel you're looking to do. I'd be sorry if you got stuck out there in the mountains on account of low clearance. That Ford truck at the end of the lot might be better suited to those rutty country roads."

"If that doesn't make perfect sense, I don't know what does."

Hedsel looked relieved.

"Oh, I'm glad. I thought maybe you had your heart set on one of these here coupes."

"To be honest, I prefer a truck. I drive one back home."

"And where would that be?"

"Virginia. Just outside Alexandria."

"I've got a cousin in Falls Church. You know it?"

"Sure, I know it. Small world, like they say."

Hedsel found an ink pen in the sill of the kiosk and tapped it on the signature line of the rental agreement.

"Sign here, and she's yours for the week."

Charlie signed and took the keys. He thanked Hedsel, but before he could reach the truck, the fat man called to him.

"There's one thing I wanted to mention, if it's not a bother."

Charlie set his luggage in the bed of the truck and turned around.

"What is it?"

"It probably don't even need to be mentioned, but the folks up there in the mountains, well." He stood thoughtfully with his hands cupped in the air as if waiting for the right words to fall in. "They're great people. Salt of the earth. But they can be suspicious of government folks."

Charlie grabbed Hedsel's shoulder reassuringly.

"Larry, you're a good man. I appreciate the advice. But I know what I'm getting into."

"Well, I thought you did. Like I said, it probably didn't need to be mentioned. Just that my first thought when I heard a USDA man was coming to Ashe County was *dear Lord send your angels.*"

"I'm not here to shut anybody down. Just research."

"I didn't mean anything by it." He slipped a business card from his breast pocket and wrote a number on the back of the card. "If I'm not at home, I'm here babysitting these Fords. Call me if there's anything I can do for you."

He drove the next block to the Jefferson Hotel, a squat two-story brick building with long streetside windows and white balustrades. From a bar across the street, men in gabardine shirts and wide-brimmed hats stopped their conversations and watched him pull the truck to the curb. Charlie tipped his hat and they did the same, smoking and shuffling their feet in the bright morning light. In the hotel lobby, he was greeted by a short brunette with a dark grey mole on her eyelid that made her look somewhat cockeyed. She gave a friendly smile and looked him over with more interest than he was prepared for.

"You must be the young man from Alexandria," she said. There was a little wink in her voice, but perhaps her eye just made it seem that way. "You come down on the Creeper?"

"Yes, ma'am. Straight shot from Abingdon Station."

"Then you must have taken a different train. Nothin' straight about gettin' to West Jefferson."

"To be honest, I think I left my stomach somewhere at the state line."

She took another survey from head to toe and gave a quick snort.

"My name's Deedee in case you were plannin' on introducin' yourself."

"I was just getting around to it."

"Don't let me stop you, honey."

"Charlie Danwitter. Pleased to meet you."

"What you ain't got in manners you got in good looks, Mr. Danwitter. Lord knows there ain't enough blue-eyed men in this world."

"If we're friends now, you can call me Charlie."

She gave a satisfied look and gathered a handful of papers from a darkwood mail sorter behind her and had him sign and initial for the room. Then she handed him a key with a polished steel fob that read 212.

"There's a telephone in the room that'll call the front desk. Whoever is here at the time can connect you to a local number. Now, if you need a long-distance number, there's a pay phone on the street you can use. It takes change but it don't take pennies—so don't try."

"I can't call Washington from the room?"

"They don't speak English in Virginia? I said quite plainly that you need to use the payphone for that, sweetheart."

He took out his wallet and opened the billfold.

"Well in that case, do you have change for a dollar? I'll need to call my boss this afternoon."

She lifted an eyebrow and her mole seemed to darken a shade.

"I can do it, but I typically don't keep a lot of change in this here register. If you're plannin' to use the payphone, I'd recommend a visit to the bank down the street. With all the dimes they got there, you could call Italy and talk to the Pope."

He handed her a dollar and she gave him back an assortment of change. He thanked her and hoisted his luggage.

"Sorry we don't have anyone to help with your luggage at the moment," said Deedee. "Our bellboy is sick today. Or maybe he's just out huntin'. It'll be a late harvest moon this week and it's kind of a big deal around here if you didn't know it. Just wait and see. Every damned truck will have a rack of antlers peekin' out by the end of the week. Best I can do is follow you upstairs and make sure you get into your room okay."

"Why don't I just holler if I need you?"

"I'll keep an ear out, Charlie."

The room was small, with just enough space for a twin bed atop an old country bed frame, a chest of drawers, and a writing desk. A candlestick telephone sat on a bedside table beside a glass ashtray. Charlie set his bags by the bed and went to the window.

Across the street was a hardware store with pegboards full of hammers and woodsaws in the windows and other out-of-place items like alarm clocks and birdcages. A sale on lightbulbs for ten cents apiece.

Gopher traps went for a dollar. He spotted the Bell telephone booth on the corner of Main and Jefferson. If he leaned far enough out the window he could see the bar cattycorner to the payphone.

He sorted his clothes into the chest of drawers and when he was unpacked, he sat on the edge of the bed and fell onto the comforter. His thoughts adrift, he blinked at the tin ceiling. The room smelled faintly of dust, and it made him wonder how long the room had been vacant. Over the window frames, someone had painted a simple fresco of two blossoming fruit tree branches crisscrossing each other with an insect stamped over the pink petals. A moth, maybe. Or a bee. He could almost see it crawling from flower to flower. Tiny antennae wavering. Wings buzzing.

The phone rang, startling him.

He answered on the third ring, announcing himself by first and last name.

"Charlie, it's Deedee. Down at the front desk."

"Hello, Deedee. Checking up on me already?" He tapped out a cigarette from a pack in his breast pocket and lit it.

"Just a courtesy call. I been listenin' to the radio and they said rain's comin' our way tonight. Could be a regular frog strangler. Thought you should know in case it interfered with your business plans."

"That's very kind of you. How bad will it get?"

"They say if it's sprinklin' in Charlotte, it's floodin' in Ashe County."

"So you expect it to flood?"

"It's just a sayin'. But I do expect it to get wet."

"I see. Well, I expected a little weather this time of year."

"Sometimes we get a lot of weather. I lost a sister this time seven years ago. Swept up in the river and never found. Rest her soul."

"I'm sorry."

"She was one of the good ones. Not many of those left."

She hung up and Charlie stood smoking for a moment. He ashed the cigarette into the tray beside the phone and glanced at the painted insect above the window. He watched it for a long while and then he picked up the receiver and dialed zero on the rotary. Deedee answered instantly.

"Say, Deedee. How is the food at the bar across the street?"

"You talkin' about The Old Gambit?"

"The one right across the street."

"You'd be likelier to find a fistfight than a good meal. Maybe a side of venereal disease."

"That bad?"

"I'd stick to Mac's Diner. They're just a block down and mostly free of drunks and whores. At least the obvious ones. People come from as far as the coast for their apple pie. Bring me back a slice and I'll pay you for it."

He donned his coat and went down to the street. It was midday, a slight wind in the trees. Warm sun and cool air. An older Ford wheeled slowly onto Jefferson and he watched the driver crane his neck to the window and spit a ropey black wad onto the street as he passed. A pickup followed not far behind with a load of squabbling fowl in wood-slat cages. Wings pumping and settling. Downy feathers whirling over the street like wood ash. He waited on the curb until the road cleared and then he crossed the street to the telephone booth on the corner and lifted the receiver to his ear. The operator instructed him to insert twenty cents for the call. The phone rang and a woman's voice answered.

"Barb, it's me. Charlie."

"Oh, Charlie, how's your trip? Made it in one piece?"

"Yes, I did. I'm calling to check in. Is Hostetter around?"

"He's in a meeting now."

"In a real meeting, or is he just taking a nap? Be honest."

Barb giggled.

"I won't tell him you said that."

"You can tell him, I don't mind. Well, what is it?"

"It's a real meeting, Charlie. He's on the phone with the big boss."

"Secretary Brannan?"

"Well, it's not Truman, silly. I have a message I'm supposed to read to you in case he couldn't take your call. Would you like me to read it to you?"

"I'm all ears."

"It's from Hostetter. He says: 'The White House has taken an interest in your assignment. Secretary Brannan mentioned it yesterday in a cabinet meeting and it stirred up a lively discussion. More funding is likely for equipment upgrades and travel. Unfortunately, your counterpart in West Virginia has been unsuccessful thus far and we are pulling him from the field.'"

"Is he talking about Gibbets?"

"Yes, unfortunately."

"What do you mean 'unfortunately'? What happened?"

There was a pause.

"He didn't want me to say."

"You can tell me, Barb."

Another pause.

"He was assaulted, Charlie." She was whispering now. "His correspondence stopped and then he turned up in a hospital in Charleston. That's all I know. Please don't say you heard it from me."

"Assaulted by whom?"

"Hostetter thinks it's the locals. Nobody knows but Gibbets, and he hasn't recovered yet."

The operator came on and asked for more change. Charlie thumbed another dime into the slot.

"Is there more to the message?"

"Yes. It says: 'Please begin work immediately upon arrival and expedite all field reports. This is no longer a pet project, but a topic of growing interest in Washington.' That's all of it. Oh, Charlie, please be careful down there."

"I'll be fine, Barb. Everyone is friendly so far."

"I hope that's true."

"Do me a favor, though. If you get any details on Gibbets, please call me at the hotel."

"I'll see what I can do."

He set the receiver in the cradle. It was warm inside the telephone booth. He took off his coat and hung it in the crook of his arm. He lifted the receiver again and dialed the operator. He asked for Charleston, West Virginia, and added the rest of the change from his pocket. The line clicked and hummed. Another operator answered and it sounded like she was speaking through a thousand miles of wire.

"Can you please connect me to the main hospital in Charleston?" asked Charlie.

"You want St. Francis, sir?"

"Yes, that'll do."

The line pulsed again. A woman from the hospital answered and asked how she could direct the call.

"Do you have a current patient named Gibbets?" asked Charlie. "Martin Gibbets?"

"Givens?"

"No, Gibbets." He spelled it out.

There was a long silence.

"Are you a relative of Mr. Gibbets, sir?"

"No, ma'am. I'm a work colleague from the USDA. I just need you to leave a message to have him call me when he's able. It's an urgent matter."

"I'm afraid I can't do that, sir."

"Why not?"

The sound of a long breath distorted the line.

"I'm sorry, sir. Mr. Gibbets passed this morning."

He was coming back from lunch at Mac's Diner when a woman called to him. She was standing in the doorway of the Old Gambit, leaning into the jamb, smoking a cigarette. Blonde, mid-twenties. She wore a dull grey apron over a low-hemmed flower-print dress.

"That a slice of pie from Mac's?" she asked.

Charlie hoisted the box as if trying to remember where he'd bought it.

"Sure is. The hotel clerk had me bring her a slice."

"You stayin' at the Jefferson?" She pointed her chin at the hotel.

"Yes, ma'am."

"Do me a favor and tell Deedee it wouldn't hurt to send a few hungry men our way now and then." She folded her arms and raised a slender eyebrow. "Lord knows I make a better pie."

"If I'm honest, this one was a little tart for my taste."

"I bet I can be twice as honest."

"How's that?"

"Those pies taste like dogshit."

Charlie laughed.

"It wasn't quite that bad."

He could see a few dark figures shifting in the gloom behind her. Hank Williams played on the radio and there were sounds of a cue ball clattering over a pool table. Blue smoke curtained the air like strange weather.

"You want to know the secret to a good, sweet pie?" she said.

"Tell me."

She laced her arms tighter around her chest.

"Sweet apples."

"That should've been my first guess."

He introduced himself and she regarded him with a coy once-over. She said her name was Cal and that she and her brother ran the place together. She did the cooking and the waitressing, and he ran the bar.

"How long are you in town?" she asked.

"A few days. Maybe longer."

"Just enough time to cause a ruckus."

"A ruckus is the last thing I need."

"Well then. It's good to meet you, Charlie Danwitter," she said. "I can't yet tell if this town is more or less interesting with you in it. Why don't you come by later for a drink and we'll find out? If you're lucky, I'll let you taste my pie."

He delivered the apple pie to Deedee and went straight to his room, where he shut the drapes and began sorting his equipment into a small duffel. He unpacked a Revere 88 from a padded case and butterflied the film compartment open and he loaded a roll of Kodachrome 8 mm film onto the feeder pin. When he'd fed the film through its labyrinth of gears and fastened it to the take-up spool, he closed and locked the compartment and began loading another roll of Kodachrome into a 35 mm Kodak Rangefinder. He packed everything into the duffel and opened the drapes.

The wind had picked up, but the sky was mostly clear and blue. It was one-thirty in the afternoon, and he figured there'd be just enough time to survey the first orchard on the list before evening fell and the rain caught up to him.

He steered the truck northward along a paved logging road that snaked through dark and barren hills where every so often a lone oak or hickory hung, choking on ivy. He passed the ruins of an abandoned lumber mill. Collapsed A-frames and corrugated awnings lay twisted and decayed. Piles of busted concrete heavy with weeds. A coal-black rockface rose and fell beside the road. An ancient lava bed now slantwise and veiled beneath shrub roots and vines.

At the town of Warrensville, the road forked north and west. He hooked westward beneath a stand of black walnut trees where he could hear birds calling from the canopies. After another mile, he pulled onto a rut road and consulted a map and deemed he was exactly where he expected to be. There was a healthy apple orchard on the opposite side of a narrow creek, branches laden with fruit. Soon the road opened to a circular driveway with a bramble of rhododendrons in the center.

An old clapboard farmhouse squatted at the far end of the drive. He parked the truck and went to the front door with the duffel over his shoulder and knocked. No answer. He waited a minute and knocked again. A dog howled distantly but there was no movement inside the house. He ambled along the banks of the creek and came to a weathered stone bridge, just wide enough for a wagon or a small automobile. He crossed to the other side and stood marveling at the orchard. Maybe a hundred trees in rows of ten. The fruit was crimson-colored, fading to a pinkish ombre at the calyx. He kneeled in the clover and found a fallen apple there, turned it over in his hands. A constellation of blonde lenticels freckled through the skin. He set the duffel beside him and unlatched the canvas flap. As he was setting the aperture on the Rangefinder, the sound of a two-stroke tractor engine came sputtering through the trees. He waited. The tractor motored over the stone bridge and came slowly toward him. An old man with a brittle straw hat, an equally old dog seated at his feet.

Charlie stood ready with a big smile.

"Howdy," he called to the man.

The man cut the engine and sat watching him through the rheum of his ancient eyes. Half of his bottom lip had been cut away and a dark brew of tobacco juice seeped through the pickets of his teeth. He spat and wiped his exposed gums with the palm of his hand and smeared the mess on his overalls.

"Whatcha got in that poke?" asked the old man.

"Poke?"

"You sassin' me?"

Charlie sensed a dark tone. He offered up the Kodak for the old man's inspection. "It's just a camera, sir. I'm from the—"

"I said what's in the poke. I can see what's in your hand."

Charlie glanced at the small duffel at his feet. "There's an eight-millimeter camera inside."

"Eight of what, now?" The man spoke loudly and it made the dog nervous. The animal groaned and licked its snout.

"It's just another camera."

"You ain't stealin my apples are you?"

"No sir, I wouldn't dream of it. Did you get my letter? You're Mr. Munroe aren't you? I'm Charlie Danwitter with the U.S. Department of Agriculture."

"Say you are?"

"The USDA. From Washington. I wrote to you last month."

"You can get back there, too. Right quick."

Charlie took a deep breath and gathered himself. He straightened his tie and set his smile hard in the jaw.

"I think we got off on the wrong foot," he said. He held his hand out thumb-skyward and stepped toward him. Munroe reared up and sent the dog scrambling to the ground. From behind his seat, he brought a double-barrel shotgun to his shoulder and rested the barrels on the steering wheel. Charlie let the camera fall to the dirt and held up his hands.

"I don't mean to cause trouble," said Charlie.

"Well." He spat and made a gesture as if he didn't have a say in the matter. "I'm afraid my twelve gauge does intend to cause a little bit of trouble."

"Please, Mr. Munroe. I'd like to introduce myself properly."

"Maybe you can write me another letter."

"Did you read the one I sent?"

"Reckon I wiped my ass with it." The old man thumbed the hammers on the shotgun and spat. "Get your shit and get off my property."

Charlie gathered the duffel and scooped the camera out of the dirt. The dog growled as he inched around the tractor, blind-looking eyes casting about.

"I sure would be happy with just an apple off the ground," said Charlie. He could hear the desperation in his own voice. "Just something to take back with me and write up a quick assessment. I'd pay you for it."

"Pay me how much?"

"I'd pay two dollars for it."

"For a felled apple?"

"That's right. I'd pay five if you told me the variety."

"I know'd they all gone loony in Warshington."

Charlie slowly took out his wallet and thumbed five dollars in ones from the billfold. He held the bills in the air and gestured pleadingly at the apple tree.

"Give the money to the dog," said Munroe.

"Excuse me?"

"It's a trick I teached him."

"You want me to give it to him how?"

"Jus' hand it to him. He know what to do."

Charlie cautiously approached the dog and offered the money.

"You got to get close. He can't see well."

When the dog caught sight of the cash, it snapped the bills and held them up to the sky with its snout quivering. It whined and shook. A puddle of urine spread beneath the animal as if the tension had overwhelmed its bladder.

"That's a pretty good trick," said Charlie.

"It's the only reason I ain't shot him yet."

Charlie went to the apple tree and picked the fallen apple out of the clover.

"So what do you call it?" he asked.

"I call it Bullet and that's what it's gonna get in a week or two."

"I meant the apple."

"The apple?"

"What do you call it at market?"

"Oh. She's an Ashe Pippin."

The wreck of his bottom lip made his response sound like a curse word.

"I didn't hear that, Mr. Munroe."

"An Ashe Pippin, I say."

"Thank you. If it's worth it to you, I'd pay another five dollars to photograph your orchard with my movie camera. Maybe take a soil sample and some tree measurements. It wouldn't take long."

Munroe bristled.

"I've had enough of all this foolery. I'm a busy man, dammit."

"You wouldn't take any money for it?"

"Yessir I would. But you'd tell all your gov'mint friends about my farm and next thing ol' Munroe's got a tax bill in the mail. Wouldn't be no five-dollar tax, neither. More like a hunnerd and five."

"Sir, I'm not a tax assessor of any kind."

"So you say. Well, I ain't a fool. Devils, the lot of you. Curled up in your warrens of sin and filth. Forked peckers drazzlin' the eyes of the common man. Suppin' on the blood of babes. This here mongrel's got more godliness than your kind and his farts would make the Lord weep and send the walls of Jericho a-tumblin'." He retrained the shotgun on Charlie. "Now get 'fore I bust you plumb out."

———

A few scattered drops of rain fell as he left Munroe's orchard, and by the time he reached West Jefferson it had developed into a full downpour. He could hardly see through the windshield with the wipers on. It was still light out, but the sky had turned a very dark grey in the rearview. He parked the truck beside the hotel and plunged shin-deep into the water accumulating on the road. He waded to the curb with his duffel and went high-stepping over the runoff. He ran dripping over the ornate carpet of the hotel lobby, hair plastered to his face.

"Sorry for the mess, Deedee," he called.

Nobody replied. The lobby was cold and quiet.

He climbed the stairs and went into his room and quickly shut the door behind him. He carefully set the telephone on the floor and moved the bedside table to the window. It was five o'clock and there was just enough daylight to photograph the Ashe Pippin. He set the aperture and snapped the first few images in profile, then two from the top at varying distances. A single leaf remained attached to the stem and he oriented its broadside to capture the verdant color and all the striated venules that came forking from the veins. He flipped the fruit onto its top and photographed the calyx beneath its rim of pinkish lobes. He'd already opened the aperture to its maximum and now the light was beginning to wane beyond the camera's capabilities. He pulled the switch cord on the desk lamp and spun the shade so the bulb stage-lit the apple on its pedestal. From the trunk of his suitcase he found a scale and quickly assembled it and weighed the fruit, committing its weight to memory. He removed a sheathed paring knife from the inside pocket of his coat and bisected the apple, and with rain spattering the window glass he photographed the starburst flesh and jet-black pentacle of seeds. When he was finished, he wound the film canister, set the Rangefinder on the desk, and fell back upon the bed. His hair was still wet from the short walk to the hotel, and it darkened the bedspread around him. He suddenly felt exhausted and lightheaded.

He looked at his watch. Still an hour left to write a summary report and get everything to the post office before it closed for the night. He felt the blood pumping throughout his body, heart banging. A nerve in his thumb began to twitch and he tried to hold it still with the opposite hand. He shut his eyes and listened to the rain.

From somewhere in the room came a faint buzzing.

He rose in the bed, tapped out a cigarette and lit it.

There it was again. A seedy vibrato that came and went.

He sat in a cloud of tobacco smoke, eyes wandering.

Then he saw it. A strange insect scaling the rim of the apple, crude antennae wavering as it went. It chittered and flicked its tiny malformed wings, winding its way to the center of the apple.

He rose to his feet and stepped closer, watching it move. It didn't look like a real insect at all, but a child's rendering of an insect, as if made of crayon-strokes. Something you'd find in an elementary school diorama. His eyes darted to the fresco above the window and his cigarette dropped to the floor.

The painted insect had disappeared from the wall.

Charlie shut his eyes and tried to calm his breath.

The chittering wouldn't stop. It was picking up, growing more excited.

He stamped out the cigarette and went to his coat where he found the vial of pills in the inside pocket. He crushed one with his back teeth and pressed the bitter slag under his tongue. He waited. Heartbeat slamming in his ears. He could see the insect making busy circles around the center of the apple as if trying to work the seeds out of the core.

Just breathe. It ain't real. Breathe.

He scooped the spent film canister from the desk and shoved it in his pocket. There was a bottle of pen ink in the drawer. He uncapped it and wet a fountain pen. Another deep breath. He could feel the barbiturate cooling his nerves even as the insect scuttled in his periphery. With a sheet of hotel stationery, he wrote a hasty note:

October 4th, 1949

Enclosed: undeveloped film of 2 ty. 1 Ashe Pippen. Specimen collected in Warrensville, North Carolina. Ashe County. 6.4 oz

Report to follow.

Inspector Charles Danwitter

He folded it, donned his coat, and slipped out the door.

The sky was nearly dark when he wandered back from the post office beneath an umbrella he'd borrowed from the hotel lobby. Steady rain, empty streets. A constant sound all around him like stadium noise. Gutters were roaring with water. He watched a dog go limping diagonally across Main and disappear into the void of an alleyway. He passed under the eaves of a shuttered Army recruitment center and briefly saw his image reflected in the window glass. The way he stood warped and backlit in the gaslamp's glow made him look extraterrestrial. Neck oddly slender, head haloed. Something from a different time and place, perhaps.

The hotel was dark when he returned. He stood in the doorway, shaking out the umbrella. At the bar across the road, he could hear country music playing. Figures smoking in the lighted windows. He glanced over the lobby at the shadowy stairwell, feet planted firmly in the jamb. He couldn't bring himself to go back to his room.

Somebody from the bar shouted. A man was cursing and staggering haphazardly in the street, going crossways through the intersection. Charlie lit a cigarette and leaned into the doorway. Another man tottered after the first and tried to throw a punch, but he only managed to knock himself off-balance and down into the muck of the street. Charlie watched as the pair regained their footing and grappled each other in a clumsy dance that looked much more affectionate than hostile. They rocked together, elbows out.

A step forward, a step back. Neither could knock the other one down.

Someone called his name.

Cal stood in the doorway of the Old Gambit, waving to him.

Charlie gave the hotel lobby another once-over, then he opened the umbrella and headed toward her. She greeted him with a bemused look.

"Did Deedee forget to pay the power bill?" she said.

Charlie shrugged.

"Haven't seen her all evening. I don't even know where the light switches are."

"Well, you won't have to find mine, honey." She took him by the hand and led him inside. "Goddamn, you look like you could use a drink. Hard day at the office?"

"You have no idea."

Cal flicked the water from the back of Charlie's coat.

"Sit down here and let Beechy pour you something."

She spun away to the back of the room and the bartender pressed his palms flat on the bar and gave Charlie a practiced smile. He was a stocky man with coarse brown hair and a square jaw that looked almost geological. A scar slanted over his left eye like a third brow, and it gave him a slightly sinister appearance despite his welcoming demeanor. He introduced himself as Beech Buchanan, Cal's older brother. Charlie returned the courtesy and they shook hands. He looked about while Beech poured two fingers of whiskey into a small glass with filmy hard water stains. The place was just large enough for a pool table, a jukebox, and the L-shaped bar that sat about ten drinkers. On the walls were old photographs of the town and pennants from local sports championships.

"I saw the fight outside," said Charlie. "Looks like you lost your two best customers."

It took a moment for Beech to register this.

"You mean Bill and Donnie? I wouldn't rightly call them our best customers. Hell, their bar tab's likely bigger than your mortgage."

"They wouldn't make any money prize-fighting, I tell you what."

"Shit. Those old boys couldn't make money any which way. If they had a roll of dimes up their assholes they still couldn't make change."

Charlie drank. The jukebox was playing Bob Wills and the Texas Playboys. Heavy fiddle filled the room. There was a spirited game of pool afoot with a stack of bills laid out on the rail. He watched them play, two spindly-legged old men with maybe a whole head of teeth between them. Swearing and hissing at the missed shots, they hooted at the sunk billiards. A couple of old whores with heavy makeup sat at the far end of the bar. They smoked and eyed him through the haze of their cigarettes.

He'd nearly finished his drink without realizing it when Beech came around and topped off the glass.

"You serve in the war?" asked Beech. "You look about the right age."

"Yes, sir. Third Armored Division."

"The famous Third Herd, huh? You boys really sent those Germans back to Kraut town."

"We did all right."

"Shit. You did more than all right, son. Stationed there long?"

"Sent home after Hürtgen on a medical discharge."

"Lord that must have been a barnburner."

"It was hell."

Beech pointed to the scar on his forehead.

"Iwo Jima. Fifth Marine Division. Took some shrapnel crossin' the island but I made it through till the end. This here town sent forty men, twenty came back. Same in 1918."

"It's always the same," said Charlie. "They keep calling and we keep shipping out."

He gave a solemn nod and raised his glass. Beech held up a finger, poured his own, and they clinked glasses and drank deeply.

Cal appeared with a steaming wooden bowl and laid it before him. From her apron she produced a spoon and a cloth napkin and set it beside the bowl. It was some kind of beef stew—carrots and potatoes in a dark broth.

"Made fresh this evenin'," she said.

"Thank you," said Charlie. He leaned in nose-first to smell the vapor welling from the bowl. "I didn't know how hungry I was."

"You'll be ready to pop when you're done. It's a hearty stew."

She had her hand on his shoulder, talking close. The quantity of booze on her breath rivaled his own.

"How much do I owe you?"

"They're charging eighty cents for it down at Mac's, but I'd take fifty. Reckon you'll take another glass of whiskey?"

"Why not?"

"Well, then. I'll even throw in a slice of pie."

"Apple pie?"

"It's apple season, ain't it?"

"Last I checked."

She flicked his shoulder.

"I promised it to you just this afternoon, don't you remember?"

"I remember. I wasn't going to hold you to it."

"Didn't want you to figure we're unfriendly people." She winked and then she stepped back, studied his face very intently. "What's that smile for?"

"It's nothing."

"Like hell it ain't."

"It's nothing, really."

"You reckon we're a bunch of mean ol' hicks?

"No. But today I almost got shot in Warrensville."

"What? What do you mean, shot?"

"I mean, almost shot with a shotgun."

Cal looked him over amusedly.

"Well, that's Warrensville for you. Nothin' but a bunch of mean ol' hicks up that way." She sat on the stool beside him with her hand covering her mouth, trying not to laugh.

"You think it's funny?"

"No, sir." She was having trouble stifling her laughing jag, water building in the corners of her eyes. "I'm just tryin' to picture you out that way with your suit and tie, getting those old farmers all hot and bothered. Probably thought you was the tax man."

Charlie ladled a small helping of stew to his lips and cooled it with a long, steady breath. He slurped at the spoonful and tossed a sideways look to see if she was still laughing. She was.

"Well, your stew is damn good," he said. "The jury's still out on your sense of humor."

"I'm just awful, I know. I can't help it."

"Mmm-hmm."

"I'm sorry. But now curiosity has taken hold of me. What the blazes were you doing out in Warrensville?"

He drank from the whiskey glass and looked thoughtfully at the remaining sip.

"I'm with the Department of Agriculture. They sent me down here on a special assignment to look for old apple orchards."

"Do what, now?"

"Apple orchards."

She straightened.

"Hear that, Beechy?"

Beech wandered down the bar and whipped a moist rag over his shoulder.

"Hear what, now?"

"Charlie's down here looking for old apple orchards."

The siblings exchanged glances.

"Now what do you want with an old apple orchard?" asked Beech.

"Well. Some people in Washington worry the country's moving too fast toward factory farming. Someday soon you might only have three or four varieties of apples to choose from, all of them from big companies."

"Sounds like plenty."

"Let him talk, Beech," said Cal.

"I mean three or four varieties across the whole country. So the small-time farmers go out of business, cut down their orchards, and these old varieties will go extinct. Nobody will ever know what an Ashe Pippin tastes like again. It'll probably happen anyway, but some of the old-timers at the USDA want to see what's out there in case there's a chance to save them."

"Lord, you come a long way from soldierin'," said Beech.

Charlie grinned.

"Everybody needs a job, don't they?"

"Ever heard of a Red Squire?" said Cal.

"No, ma'am. That another apple variety around here?"

Beech whipped his sister playfully with the rag.

"He don't want to hear that nonsense."

"The hell he don't. He just said that's why he's here."

Charlie was already feeling a little tipsy, so he took a few big bites of stew to fill his stomach. "Tell me," he said, holding the bite in the pocket of his cheek. "Lord knows I need all the help I can get around these parts."

"Set us up with another round, Beechy."

"I don't know if I should have another," said Charlie.

"Just drink with me."

Beech poured two glasses, then shook his head and wandered down the bar.

"He don't like when I talk about it," she said.

"Why?"

"I'll tell you why. Our granddad come from this village up along the Tennessee line. A little place called Wyldton. I'll give you a million dollars if you can find it on a map. Nice folks, but a little funny in their ways."

"Funny how?"

"You're not one to let a lady talk? I'm trying to explain it to you. See, our grandad was full of crazy stories about growing up there, and he'd take us some years for the apple harvest festival. There's lots of drinkin' and dancin' and things you maybe wouldn't see from regular Christian folks. Beech thinks it's all silly."

"What do you mean they're not regular Christians?"

"Reckon they're Christians, just kinda peculiar ones."

"And the apple variety they harvest is called a Red Squire?"

She let her hand rest on his leg.

"Look at you, all ears about it."

"Like you said earlier. Curiosity has taken hold of me."

"I like a man who can pay attention."

He put his hand on hers and she gave a broad smile.

"Go on, please," he said.

"The children sing a song about it. When they sing it in the orchard during the festival, they're given sweet cider to drink." She looked briefly at the ceiling as if putting the words together in her mind. Then she danced her fingers over the bar in a miniature performance. "The raven spread her wings o'black, the jack leapt from the briar." She walked her fingers slowly toward him. "The buck did raise his thorny rack, and bit that old Red Squire!" She darted her fingers to his hand as if taking a bite, then scurried back again and gave a bow.

Beech rushed over, brows knitted.

"Come on, Cal. Why you gotta sing that in here?" His eyes darted from one end of the room to the other. "It's childish."

"Why you so sore about it? Charlie wanted to know."

"Well maybe Charlie wants to eat his stew."

"It's okay," said Charlie. "Maybe we can talk about it another time."

"See," said Beech. "He wants to talk about it another time."

Cal drank the rest of her drink in one sip and folded her arms.

"I'm sorry my brother's such a grump."

"I'll show you a grump."

"Well, I meant asshole." She walked off with her middle finger out and her tongue wagging as she went.

Beech cleaned the bar around Charlie's place setting.

"Sorry about her," he said. "She can be a little chatterbug. I've a mind to teach her a thing or two."

"It's fine. Like I said before, I'm here to find old orchards."

"Well, move Wyldton to the bottom of your list. Plenty of old orchards just around the bend without having to truck all the way to the Tennessee line."

"When was the last time you saw that old village?"

"It's been years. I'd be surprised if anyone still lived there to be honest. I wouldn't waste my time if I was you."

It was after midnight when Charlie stepped half-drunk from the doorway of the Old Gambit with an unlit cigarette dangling in the corner of his mouth. He looked up and down the empty road. A bicycle with a raincoated rider jangled down Jefferson. Dim reflections danced in the wet of the street. He watched a woodrat scurry into the lamplight and rear onto his haunches, pawing its human-like digits as if climbing an invisible ladder. It twitched its nose in the light rain and turned loping down the sidewalk toward the center of town. The hotel windows hung black in their sills. The lobby, the rented rooms, all dark. He stepped off the curb and his foot went straight down into a puddle. The cigarette he'd forgotten about tumbled into the water. He caught himself and looked about with arms windmilled to see if anyone had seen him and then he shook off his wet shoe and crossed the street.

He pushed open the front door and gazed into the black of the lobby. No switches on the walls. From the light of the street, he could just make out the black and white couch with a low table on the far side, a lamp with a pull switch sitting on the table. He went slowly, hands in front like a sleepwalker. One step, then another. He banged his shin on a low table and cried out in pain.

Something clattered in the far corner of the lobby. He wasn't alone.

"That you, Deedee?" he called.

A moan. The sound of something dragging over the carpet.

An animal must have gotten in.

He pulled the beaded lamp switch and shaded his eyes at the sudden light.

There was little time to process the figure running toward him—a man of green and orange lichen. A mouth that sagged taffy-like in a pink, toothless frown, with saliva driveling from the folds. From the eyes came pinhole pupils that cast about wildly atop two translucent stalks like on a snail. Veins pumped inside those appendages. He could see the ink-black blood moving up and down the stalks from within. It looked like an amalgam of every orchard pest he'd ever seen, and it charged right into him.

The impact knocked him off his feet. Charlie careened shoulder-first onto the hardwood floor and took a hard punch to the jaw. Vision gone bone-white, a frenzy of light particles zagged through the scene. He held up his hands to stop another blow and blinked through his splayed fingers at the crazed demonic figure. A sick smell of compost welled over him and he arched his shoulders and gagged at the stench. The creature moaned and hit him again. He felt wet tentacles over his chin and mouth, then his throat. Maybe they were roots.

Charlie managed to slip a hand into the inside pocket of his coat.

He found the cool heaviness of the paring knife inside.

He was choking now.

He hauled back and jammed the knife into the thing's side, but it had no effect. He jammed again and looked. The knife was still sheathed in its little wooden scabbard. The room tunneled, and his fingers were going numb. He slipped the knife between his thigh and the floor and tilted with whatever weight he could put on it. When he lifted the blade again, the sheath stayed pinned beneath him and he jabbed with the naked blade.

The thing howled and loosened its grip.

He gasped and stabbed twice more.

The creature fell back scrabbling over the low table. It screeched and moaned and stumbled to the front door and out into the night. Charlie rolled onto his chest and pushed himself up, all shaking hands and aching jaw. His throat felt hot and tender. At the window he could just make out a humanoid shadow cutting into the alley beyond the hardware store and out of sight.

He staggered through the lobby and found the telephone on Deedee's reception desk and dialed the operator. It took a few tries to connect. His fingers were shuddering in the track of the rotary. The room still smelled of that sickening rot and it was all he could do to keep from vomiting. When the operator came on the line, he asked to be patched through to the police, and when they answered he gave a sanitized version of what happened. They told him to lock the place up and they'd send someone as soon as they could.

The sheriff didn't arrive until morning.

Charlie spent the night in his locked room with the paring knife curled in his fingers, listening to every creak and moan in the walls of the old hotel. Somehow in the scuffle, he'd lost his medication and he could feel every nerve in his body. When a knock on the door finally came, he answered with the knife clutched behind his back.

The sheriff stood in the doorway: a tall, clean-shaven man who looked either prematurely grey or youthful for his age. His immaculate tan and green uniform hinted at a military past. He was about to introduce himself when Deedee rushed through with the flair of a stage actor. She studied him wide-eyed with her hands cupped to her mouth as if stifling a scream.

"Oh, Charlie, just look what they done."

"I've been through worse. I'll be all right."

"My little sister crashed her car in the storm yesterday afternoon and I was tendin' to her children. I was so scared for her that I just ran out in a panic. I feel downright awful for leavin' you, Charlie."

The sheriff gave a flash of annoyance and cleared his throat.

"Oh, I'm just a hot mess, ain't I? Charlie, this is Sheriff Dave Danaver."

Danaver eased into the room with a hand outstretched and Charlie shook it.

"Looks like you got an ass-whuppin', son," said the sheriff. He was eyeing the knife in Charlie's other hand.

"Not so bad. Like I said, I've seen worse."

"I believe it. Word is you fought in Europe."

"Word spreads fast around here."

"I ain't much for gossip, Charlie. Don't want to give you that impression. Just part of the job, I suppose. Seems it's somethin' we have in common, anyway. By that I mean war, not gossip."

"You don't say?"

"Yessir, I do. Nineteen eighteen. Belleau Wood. I wasn't quite old enough to enlist so I lied about my age. A lot of us did back then, although I'd advise a youngster against it. Real wicked shit, as you well know. No place for a child. They used to call it the Great War but that's changin'. I still can't get used to callin' it World War I. Like it was just the first in a series. Let's just hope there ain't a third."

"Amen."

Charlie set the paring knife on the telephone table.

"You're pretty good with that thing, ain't you?" said Danaver.

"What thing?"

"The knife."

"Why do you say that?"

He glanced at Deedee.

"Could you give us a moment alone, please?" She nodded and left the room and Danaver shut the door behind her. In his hand was a leather folio. "I don't go around showin' these kinds of photos to just anyone, but I know you seen worse. Go ahead and look."

Inside were photographs of a man slumped against a brick wall, sitting in a puddle of blood. Eyes fixed and lips parted in that ponderous attitude of the dead. The photograph looked to have a strong vignette as if taken in the dark with a bright flash. Another print was closely framed to the dead man's face. Late thirties, shaggy beard. Dirt or blood smudged over his cheeks. No teeth that he could see from the slight part of his lips.

"Garbage collector found him early this mornin' just a few blocks away. I had the photographs rushed so I could bring them to you. Take a good look. Is that the party in question, Mr. Danwitter?"

Charlie studied the photograph and briefly closed his eyes. His left hand began to shake and he stuffed it in his pocket. "I'll be honest with you, Sheriff. It was dark and he caught me by surprise. I didn't get a good look."

"You got close enough to stab him with that little pigsticker. Ain't that what you said on the phone? Can't be much of a coincidence this man been stuck three times and bled out."

"Could be him. How'd he smell?"

"Do what, now?"

"How'd he smell? The guy who attacked me smelled absolutely putrefied."

"Can't say I smelt him. No bed of roses, I bet."

"When it was on top of me, I could hardly breathe on account of the stench alone. Almost enough to make me lose my stomach."

"It? You're talkin' about a man and not an animal, ain't you? Because we've got to be clear about that."

"Of course. It was a man."

"Was it this man?"

"Could be. You fellas know who this is? Was he a local?"

The sheriff gave a frustrated look and took the folio back. "One of my deputies says he might have seen him down in Beaver City. Just a tramp followin' the railroad tracks to who knows where. Do you recollect his height or weight? Color of his hair? I got to be honest with you, I thought this would be easy, son."

"I'd say he was about my height and build. We were evenly matched."

"Well at least that checks out. And the hair?"

"Wild. Sort of shaggy. Maybe he had leaves in his hair."

"And how much did you drink last night at the Gambit?"

Charlie folded his arms.

"Don't be offended," said Danaver. "Like I said, it's my job to go around askin' questions. Besides, I keep Beech and Calypso Buchanan on a mighty tight leash. You tie one on last night, Charlie?"

"Suppose I had about the right amount."

Danaver tried to hold his official persona, but a smile broke through.

"Been a while since I had the right amount. Wife won't allow it in the house. She's what you call a tee-totaler."

"I suppose you could steal a nip here and there."

"I've done it once or twice. Hard to get away with it, though. A bloodhound, that one. She could smell a drop of whiskey on the moon." Danaver tucked the folio under his arm and stuck a hand in his pocket. When he pulled it out again, he was holding a little glass vial. "You know what Nembutal is?"

Charlie froze.

The bottle was empty.

"Sounds familiar. What's it for?"

"Goofballs," said the sheriff. He read the label studiously as if for the first time. "That's what the tramps and hobos call it. We found it on the body. Take it with a cheap bottle of wine and it really slams your dick in the dirt, pardon the vulgarity. Has legitimate purposes, too. Doctors prescribe it all the time to veterans who can't shake the war jitters."

The two men locked eyes, each one reading something unspoken.

"It's mine," said Charlie. "I don't like to admit it, but it's mine."

Danaver nodded solemnly. "No shame in it, son. I've seen boys do worse when they come back. There's a reason my wife don't let me drink no more."

"I imagine that little bottle helps your case, doesn't it?"

"Damn near seals it."

"Well, then I'm glad I could help."

"Small towns don't like mysteries. Drives everyone plumb crazy. Like pissin' on an ant hill. But now we have a story. This fella come up along the railroad tracks and found an empty hotel and attempted a burglary. You catch him in the act and the situation escalates. He takes your pills, you stab him in the gut, and our fella slithers off into the night and bleeds out. Maybe with a stomach full of goofballs to hasten his ultimate demise."

"Nice work, Sheriff. If you'll excuse me, I have to find a way to salvage my assignment here. Turning up all over the county looking like I lost a fight isn't going to help me much."

"Shit, son. From what I heard around town, it could only improve your situation. To these ol' farmers, a fresh-faced government man in a suit is a thing of nightmares." Danaver turned to open the door but paused with his hand on the knob. "Anythin' else you want to add? Any details you think I'd find useful? The county coroner is a real uptight son of a bitch and I'd rather not have to track you down a second time."

Charlie shook his head and looked at his shoes, both hands now tucked beneath his arms to hide the tremors. The way Danaver's eyes were on him, he doubted his busted nerves had gone unnoticed.

"It all happened just as I told you," said Charlie.

———

He found a drug store three blocks away between a shuttered auto repair shop and a bakery. He pushed through the doors. It was still early, and the new light was falling slantwise through the windows. A little bell jingled once and then again when the door shut behind him. He glanced around the room for a clerk or pharmacist but there was no one about. A soda bar ran along the side of the room flanked by vacant padded stools with wicker backs. He fingered through a rack of newspapers and found yesterday's edition of the *Charlotte Observer*. Riots in New York City. A train crash in California. Truman was due at the outpost in Fort Bragg for an Army inspection.

An old man appeared at the back of the store. He came from a doorway that Charlie had not noticed. His white hair crested wildly over the dome of his head as if he had just woken from a long sleep. His eyes were cavernous and shadowy in that way old age erodes into frailty. He had a big white mustache with a bright orange tobacco stain at the center.

"Can I help you?" said the old man.

Charlie folded the paper and set it back carefully.

"Yes, sir, good morning. Hoping you could fill a prescription. I'll need it back quickly if it's not too much trouble."

"Show me the 'script and I'll see what I can do."

"I don't have it with me. I'm here on business."

The old man regarded him curiously.

"Say, you in a car accident?"

"A robbery. That's why I'm here."

"Oh good Lord in heaven, how terrible. Must have been a large fella by the looks of it. Where'd you get robbed, son?"

"Down the street at the Jefferson Hotel."

The old man reeled back a step with his hands covering his face.

"Oh, sweet Jesus. I'd never wager it could happen here. Satan's got his claws dug deep in this world, son. Deeper and deeper each and every year. Demons abound. They've found their way to Ashe County. Soon we'll be pawns in Beelzebub's wicked plan."

Charlie took an interest.

"Demons?"

"Never heard of 'em? Dark and tricky spirits that roam the earth and answer to Satan alone. Got a cousin out in Wagoner who does the Lord's work. Baptizin' the unwarshed right there in the New River. They call it the New River, but a newspaperman told me it's one of the oldest rivers on God's green earth. Might as well call it the Jordan. Just a quick dip in those ol' waters and you'll be steady as a preacher's hand I tell you what. That'll scour the demon stank off you, son. Warsh it clean off. That is, until the corrosion sets in once more, slowly but surely. Folks think you can bathe in the Lord's waters once and be done with it. Well maybe that's how it used to be. Hellfire. The way the world is now, you can't stroll from one end of town to the other without gettin' the stank all over again. Oh Lord, ain't it a mighty stench? Often I wonder if demons is born straight from the Devil's asshole."

Charlie shuffled his feet uncomfortably.

"When I was robbed last night, the man stole my medication. Hoping you can fill it for me today if possible."

"What's it called?"

"Nembutal. One and a half grains. A dozen capsules if possible, but I'd take what you could give me."

"Well, I don't carry it here. I could order it up from Charlotte and have it in a couple days. Make up your mind quick. I'm fixin' to close up shop for the day."

Charlie shook his head.

"No, that just won't do. I need something today. The sooner the better." He felt his brow twitch, and he discreetly rubbed his eye to calm the nerve. "Do you carry anything similar, something you can fill while I wait?"

"What seems to be the ailment?"

Charlie struggled with an answer.

"Can't sleep, is it? Got a nervous mind?"

"Something like that."

"What now?"

"It's related."

"Related to who?"

"Nervousness. And sometimes I see—"

He couldn't finish the thought.

"See what, son?"

"It's not important. I just need your help as quickly as possible."

"Get yourself to my cousin, the right Reverend Broyhill. Got himself a little shack church with a pinewood steeple right on the river."

"I'm here on business, sir. I have daily commitments."

"What other business is there than the Lord's business? I'm headed that way directly. You can ride with me."

"My work wouldn't allow it."

The old man hung his head. "Just ain't Christian. Who's your employer, son?"

"I work for the federal government."

"Well don't that say it all?"

Charlie slipped a small pad of paper from his pocket and began to write.

"I'm giving you my doctor's information. His name is W.J. Young and he's a very reasonable man. Once you sort it out, please hurry the prescription. I'll pay double the price."

"Double the price?"

"That's right."

"I ain't told you the original price."

Charlie laid a ten dollar bill on the counter.

"I'd appreciate anything you could do for me. I really need your help, Mr.—"

"Halbert."

"Mr. Halbert. I'm Charles Danwitter. So you'll call him?"

"God willin'."

"Does that mean yes?"

"Means what it means, I suppose."

Charlie closed his eyes and tried to calm his nerves. "I'll be back Friday morning," he said. "If there's any trouble with the order, please call me at the Jefferson."

He drove out past Smethport and down Buffalo Creek Road. Past wheat fields and tilted barns. Old farmhouses anchored to the hillsides under autumn-colored trees. There was a creek that ran along the road and every so often it whitened over a riffle of fallen branches. Boys lurked in tattered overalls, sitting on footbridges with fishing lines tethered to the dark streampools. Their eyes followed him on the road as he passed, the mirthful glow of youth showing through the grime.

He visited three apple orchards and he was chased off every single one.

The last of the three, he'd nearly gotten mauled by a pack of Dobermans. He ran with his heels kicking dust and leaped horizontally into the bed of the pickup. They scrabbled their black claws at the sheet metal and blew jets of steam from their snouts and from their throats came wild frenzied sounds. He lay with his arms crossed, stone-still, watching the remnants of yesterday's storm roll across the sky. Deep, even breaths. The movement of clouds brightened and darkened his face in a slow strobe. He thought they looked like strange gods staring down at him. The dogs bounced around the truck snarling and flinging drool until a fat man with a Winchester rifle on his shoulder settled the animals and peered over the truckbed and told Charlie that he'd overstayed his welcome. In a parting shot, one of the hounds tore Charlie's leather shoe clear off his foot as he was climbing into the driver's seat to leave. The fat man recovered it and dusted it off. Little stipples dotted the shoe leather where the dog laid its teeth. Handing it through the driver window he said:

"Come around again and it'll be your ass."

It was just after sunset when Charlie walked through the doors of the Old Gambit to the sound of applause. It stunned him. He stood in the doorway, trying to read the room. The cheers spread through the tavern and soon evolved to whistling and hooting.

Beech stood behind the bar with a bottle of whiskey held high.

"Here's to Chargin' Charlie, the slayer of tramps and fascists alike!"

Charlie made his way to the bar and sat, trying not to blush. He lifted the drink Beech poured and toasted the room. The riot of cheers wouldn't stop.

"Ain't you gonna tell us about it?" said an old man sitting on the next stool over. "They say you gutted that old boy like an October buck."

Charlie nodded with whatever humility he could muster.

"I stuck him well enough, I suppose."

"Damn right you did." The old man had him by the shoulder, breath boiling with liquor. "Heard he left a trail of blood from here to Market Street. That ol' tramp messed with the wrong motherfucker, didn't he?"

Cal came out from the kitchen with a smile. She went to Charlie and straightened his tie. "I thought you didn't want to cause a ruckus," she said. "Sure sounds like a ruckus to me."

"There's been worse ruckuses," he said.

"Well, I hope you're in the drinkin' mood."

"Why's that?"

"Nobody's gonna let you spend a dime in here tonight."

"I could stand a drink or two."

"You hungry? I can get you somethin' from the kitchen."

"I never did get a chance to taste your pie."

She pulled a pack of cigarettes from his shirt pocket and put one in his lips.

"Well, soldier. Maybe tonight's your lucky night."

As the night wore on, he recounted the tale of the tramp and the paring knife many times. With each round of drinks and each newcomer to the bar he gave the story a little added flourish. The creeping through the dark, the noise in the corner. The stab, stab, stab. He played it up and nobody ever got tired of hearing about it. Sometime before midnight, Cal took him by the hand and led him through the kitchen. It was just a small square space with a pantry and a gas cookstove, a large bowl of apples on the counter. A second door led to a stairwell, and up above was a tidy loft with a bed and a sofa. She flicked on a small, shaded lamp and closed the blinds, then she untied her apron and set it on a hook.

"I'd pour you a drink, but looks like you've had plenty," she said. She turned a radio on and it started playing some old-timey band music from the twenties.

He went to loosen his tie but found that he'd already stuffed it into his pocket.

"If I tell that damn story once more in my life it'll be too soon."

"You seemed to be havin' fun."

She stood close, unbuttoning the collar of his shirt.

He took her by the waist and brought her even closer.

"So, what's the verdict?" he said.

"I didn't know there was a trial."

"When I met you, you wondered if the town was more interesting with me in it."

"Jesus. After all that, you still fishin' for compliments? Men and their egos."

"Well?"

She had three buttons undone and was kissing his bare chest.

"Reckon the jury's still deliberatin'. Might do you some good to shush and leave 'em to it."

They stood kissing and unbuttoning as the music played, their clothes pooling around their feet. She brought him to the bed and lay across it with her ash blond hair spilling over the sheets. He kissed her pale breasts, her flat stomach. The dark of her navel. On the inside of her thighs were twin moth tattoos. Eye-like features on the lower wing blades. Feathery antennae. They stood out against the white of her skin. He kissed them both a long while as she lay moaning.

"They're apple moths," she said later, in the dark.

"The tattoos?"

"Yeah. Thought you was wonderin'."

"They looked familiar," he said.

"When grandad would take us to Wyldton, there was a kind old woman who would pay us a half-penny a piece for 'em. Her name was Gertrudis and she wore these beautiful slippers made of beads and braided leather. A long dress as white as the clouds. Me and Beech would hunt the moths in the orchard and put 'em in a mason jar and the old woman would fill it with water and count their little dead bodies afterwards. Sounds cruel, but that's what she did."

"I've seen those things ruin an entire orchard."

"Reckon that's why she did it. But I started feelin' guilty about it. One day, instead of givin' her the jar, I took off down this old path that led beneath the town. They got these caves down there we weren't supposed to mess with because of bats, they'd say. I went in just as far as the light would reach. Roots danglin' like fingers. Like I'd found myself on the underside of a humongous tree. Well, I opened the jar and set it at my feet. If you never seen a hundred apple moths just a-flutterin' all around you in a big beautiful swarm, well it's a sight to see. Like a fairy tale. Most people like butterflies, but I prefer moths. I bet you probably guessed that by now. I like their little woolly bodies and feathery feelers on top. Anyhow, they made their way into the daylight, and I imagined each of 'em sayin' a little thank you on their way out."

"Did you get in trouble?"

"Never laid a hand on me. Cost me fifty cents, though."

Charlie laughed. "Sounds like money well spent."

She wept quietly in the dark.

"I didn't mean to tease you," he said.

"It's not that. Just hadn't thought about it for a while. Sometimes a memory's got a lot attached to it. Sometimes they got roots connected to other memories, don't you reckon? Or am I talkin' crazy?"

"I know that for a fact."

"That I'm crazy or the other thing?"

"The other thing. Even new memories get tangled with old memories somehow."

"Ain't it the truth?" She sat up in the dark. He could see her eyes wet and glinting with whatever light was in the room. "I could take you, you know."

"To Wyldton?"

"I've seen that fancy truck of yours. Wouldn't take long."

"It's not mine. It's from a rental agency."

"I wouldn't care if you stole it. Still runs."

"How long would it take?"

"Two hours, maybe less."

"Beech told me not to go."

"Never mind him. I've just about had it with him."

"To be honest, I could use a big win." He was now lying with his head in her lap, looking up at her. "The farmers around here have been running me off their orchards every damn time. If I don't give my boss something good, he'll fire me for sure."

"They wouldn't run you off up there. Not in Wyldton. I'll introduce you. It's been a while, but they'll remember me. I heard on the radio that it's a full moon on Friday. That's when they have their big festival. From the sounds of it, they're expectin' an eclipse this year. Maybe they got somethin' good planned. Somethin' better than usual. We could stay the night and come back in the mornin'."

"I leave on Saturday, we'd have to be back early."

"Straight shot down the mountain, Charlie. I wouldn't let you miss your train."

"Okay."

"Okay, what?"

"Okay, let's do it."

She squealed and kissed him crookedly, missing his lips.

"Meet me here Friday mornin' at ten. Oh, Charlie, you're gonna just love it up there."

They dressed and she led him back down into the kitchen and through a back door to a dank alleyway. He found one of the men from earlier in the night passed out against the wall with his pants down, snoring loudly. Charlie stood smoking at the mouth of the alley, watching the empty streets. A light fog had blown into town and was slipping between the old brick buildings.

The window above him creaked open and Cal stuck her head out.

"You better get back before Deedee comes lookin'," she whispered.

"She can look all she wants," said Charlie.

"I don't need her kind of attitude here. Just go. See you Friday."

Charlie flicked his cigarette and sent it pinwheeling into the street. He went through the intersection to the Jefferson's half-lit lobby, called to Deedee. Hearing nothing, he climbed the stairwell to his room.

He lay awake a long while, his head full of thoughts. The smell of compost from last night's attack seemed to linger in the hotel. Or maybe it was something rotting in the walls. He glanced warily about the room. Smoky images swirled in the tin ceiling. He squeezed his eyes shut and counted his heartbeats. Slow, calming breaths. He'd have to call Washington in the morning, tell them where he was headed and about all the trouble he'd faced. No doubt Hostetter would admonish him for his failures. He tried to prepare himself for the worst. At least now he had something to talk about. Something promising.

He heard the faint sound of thunder drumming at the edges of the world. He turned on his side and watched the window for lightning but saw none. When sleep finally took hold, his subconscious turned to war.

———

The men of the 22d Infantry suffered all types of weather in the Hürtgen Forest: freezing rain, dense fog, heavy snow. Mud so deep it would tear your boot clean off and fight to keep it.

On November 15, 1944, Charlie saw a worse kind of weather.

He was somewhere south of Kommerscheidt near the Siegfried Line when the lead truck struck a mine and sent half the GIs straight into the canopy, some of them dripping back down over the road in a vile rain. Pink garlands hung in the branches. Blood steamed on the icy road. A machine gun nest tore the other two trucks apart, sending Charlie with a handful of men thirty feet down the gorge and onto the banks of a half-frozen creek. Six survived the fall, some with broken arms and legs. By the time they'd found cover beneath a jumble of fallen logs, only three remained.

First Sergeant Edward Keynes was a plumber from New Jersey with a tough neighborhood accent. He had a wife and two daughters back home, and he smoked like a hot car engine on a cold day. PFC James Ratstatter was an overweight farm boy with arms like ham hocks and shifty, malevolent eyes. He looked pale and sweaty, like he was always recovering from some kind of viral infection. They spoke little under the log shelter, just listening to the sounds of high explosives rumbling through the gorge. The chatter of MG 42s obliterating the forest at twelve-hundred rounds per minute.

When the mortars changed direction, the men moved farther downstream. The canyon walls rose V-shaped above them, loose rocks zagging down the slopes with each shuddering blast. Most evenings, a dense fog would settle over the forest and obscure their positions. This evening was clear, and it was making the three of them very nervous, constantly eying the lip of the gorge for enemy soldiers.

About thirty minutes downstream, the land flattened around a brushy bend in the creek. How far they were ahead of the front lines they couldn't be certain. Keynes signaled toward a path that led through a grove of fir trees. He had an unlit cigarette in the center of his lips, and he was working it up and down as if it were doing the thinking for him.

"Count to sixty," said Keynes. "Follow me up if it's still quiet."

Charlie and Ratstatter watched him set the butt of his M1 carbine on his shoulder and step slowly up the trail. They waited, the lion's roar of mortars echoing distantly. Maybe it had been a minute, maybe less. Ratstatter gave a quick shrug and started up the trail after Keynes. Charlie followed. They stepped over roots and river stones, swept fir branches out of the path with their rifle barrels. Coming through the trees, they found Keynes crouching on one knee beside a young boy. Blond hair, mended trousers. Maybe six years old. He was frozen with fear, silently sobbing to himself, his chest jerking in a spasm. A young girl stood further up the trail, calling frantically to the boy. To the north lay a small woodshed that bowed precariously at its middle.

"Herkommen," the girl was shouting. *"Komm schon, Bruder!"*

Keynes gestured for the boy to follow her.

"Go on," he said, smiling. "Follow your sister. Go."

The boy turned woodenly in a slow semicircle and then his legs came to life. He sprinted toward the girl shrieking and crying.

Ratstatter spat.

"Shouldn't have let 'em run off, Sarge."

Keynes rose to his feet and lit the cigarette he'd been chewing on. A light snow was beginning to fall.

"What should I have done? Snapped their necks and thrown them into the water? Didn't you see the girl's basket? Just a couple of kids foraging for mushrooms."

"They're gonna say something. They won't keep quiet about it."

Keynes blew a long drag into the treetops and looked Ratstatter up and down like a bad deal. "What about you, Charlie? What would you have done?"

Charlie stood listening to the wind in the trees.

"You all right, kid?" said Keynes.

"He's shellshocked," said Ratstatter. "Had that look in his eyes since we started down the gorge."

Charlie looked up the trail where the girl had gone. He cocked his head as if he could still hear her calling. "I would have let them go," he said at last. "Sarge is right. Just a couple of kids. We won't stay long anyhow."

"You don't know where they went off to," said Ratstatter. "For all you know, Hansel and Gretel are fixin' to turn us in. Trail of breadcrumbs and all that shit. They'll lead 'em straight to us."

"Relax," said Keynes. "Listen to Charlie. We'll take shelter in that old shed and reconnect with our company in a few hours. If there's anything left of them."

There wasn't much in the shed but a few wooden crates and a small stack of cordwood against the far wall. They sat in the dim light and smoked. Ratstatter grew more restless as the minutes dragged on. He started fidgeting with the crates, then he'd sigh and suck his teeth loudly. He thumbed his lighter— a windproof Black Crackle Zippo—flicking the flame on and off in a strobe, his greasy face glowing eerily in the flamelight.

"Something on your mind?" said Keynes.

Ratstatter didn't respond. He rose in the dark and peered out into the early evening light. There wasn't much to see. A forest deep and black. Snow gathered in the field grass, whitening the boughs of the fir trees.

"I have to take a shit," he said.

"Don't go far."

He was a long time in the woods. They waited quietly, listening for sounds of his return. The forest creaked and groaned. When it seemed like thirty minutes had passed, Keynes opened the shed door and looked out. The light was failing now.

"Come with me, Charlie," he said. "We're going to look for that fat fucker. Be on your toes."

They spread out in the field, whispering Ratstatter's name into the treeline. They checked the banks of the stream and they weaved through the nearest pillars of trees. When they rejoined after a few minutes of searching, Keynes was shaking his head. He lit another cigarette and was about to say something when Ratstatter appeared at the top of the trail. He stood watching them for a moment before shuffling down, his bayoneted rifle held before him.

Keynes spat out his cigarette.

Ratstatter was covered with blood, some of it gathering at the tip of the bayonet.

"Jesus," shouted Keynes. "What the fuck happened?"

"There was a whole nest of them, Sarge. In a farmhouse up the trail." The closer he came, the more insane he looked. Blood was spattered on every inch of his uniform. On his face, down his neck. His eyes shone bright white in contrast. "We're safe now. Got 'em all."

"A nest?" said Keynes.

"Yes sir."

"You mean a family?"

"They were coming for us, Sarge."

"What about the children?"

"Sarge?"

"The children, you dumb fucking ape."

Keynes moved his hand to the Colt .45 on his belt.

"Sarge, I had to."

"No, you really didn't. That little boy didn't have a clue who we were."

"He didn't feel a thing, Sarge."

"You sick motherfucker." He pulled his sidearm, but Ratstatter was quick. The rifle shot sent Keynes staggering with his pistol falling into the grass. He briefly caught his balance, eyes searching wildly as if trying to make sense of the moment, then he fell to his knees and flat on his face.

Ratstatter swung the rifle.

"What about you, Charlie?"

Charlie had his hands in the air.

"What about me?"

"You gonna try and take me out, too?"

"Not me, James. I think you did the right thing."

He lowered his weapon.

"Thank you. I did, didn't I?"

"They would have killed us all for sure."

"You're damn right. But not anymore."

"No, not anymore."

"Sergeant Keynes almost killed me in cold blood. You saw it."

"You did the right thing, James," said Charlie. He spoke to him softly, trying to put him at ease. His eyes flicked from the bayonet and back to Ratstatter's gory face. "I'm going to put you in for a commendation when we make it back."

"Will you, Charlie?"

"Yes, sir. How far up is the farmhouse?"

"Not far. Why?"

"I need to see what you did for my commendation letter."

Ratstatter nodded enthusiastically.

"Then we'll go back?"

"Yes. I think it's safe now. Thanks to you."

"Thanks to me."

Charlie went up the trail through a dense grove of trees that gradually opened to a clearing. A farmhouse loomed in the distance, maybe a hundred yards off. The snow had let up and he could just make out the narrow path that led through the clearing, past a long bed of tilled dirt. Somewhere a horse stomped and snorted. He could smell the must of animal sweat and the bright earthy rind of manure. The farmhouse door hung halfway open, slightly crooked in the jamb. An oil lamp shifted the shadows around the small dwelling.

Charlie pushed the door with the toe of his boot. He went in rifle-first. He took two steps before he saw the pile of bodies in the adjacent room. He stood in the flickering light looking down at the horror. Arms and legs sprawled and blood-soaked. Blond hair spilling out of the mass with grey hair mixed in. A deep pond of blood encircled the pile. An iceberg of flesh in a dark black sea.

He heard a moan.

Charlie looked closer.

From the brambles of limbs, an arm reached out. Two eyes shined at him in the lamplight. It took a moment to make sense of it. A bearded face tilted from the pile like something animated from clay. A middle-aged man with a face full of blood. The arm beckoned Charlie closer. The man curled his fingers around the barrel of Charlie's rifle and gently guided it between his half-dead eyes.

"*Bitte,*" he pleaded.

Charlie jerked the rifle barrel from his grasp. The bearded man slowly reached for it again. This time,

Charlie let him take it, and the man nestled it once more into the crook of his brow. The fingers beckoned, inviting the bullet through the barrel with a grotesque hospitality.

"*Bitte.*"

Charlie trudged along the trail with the oil lamp in one hand and the rifle in the other. It was very dark now. Patches of snow glowed white in the forest silt. Where fallen branches lay across the path, he saw in their place twisted arms and legs. Where dead fir needles gathered, he saw piles of blond hair. He came through the grove and went down to the small field where Keynes lay dead in the grass. The scene was eerily peaceful. He went to the woodshed and opened the door and found Ratstatter sitting against the wall, running his fingers down the blood groove of the bayonet.

"I heard a shot," said Ratstatter. "Did you find more of them?"

Charlie nodded silently and set the oil lamp on the floor.

"Just one?"

"Just one."

"Well, then. Sounds like you got everything you needed," said Ratstatter. He hadn't bothered to clean up. He looked like some car wreck survivor who had wandered off the highway in a daze.

"Yes, James. I got what I needed."

A smile whitened Ratstatter's gruesome face.

"So you'll write the commendation?"

Charlie shook his head. "I'm afraid not."

"Why the hell not?"

"Because Keynes was right about you. You're a monster."

Before he could protest, Charlie raised the rifle to his shoulder and put a round through Ratstatter's forehead. The shot clammed his skull wide open. A ridged mollusk tongue beneath. Pink and delicate. Ratstatter's eyes went crooked and the wooden board he was leaning against shattered and fell out into the night. He settled into the break with his jaw slammed open, curtains of blood glazing his jowled and greasy face.

PART
TWO

CHARLIE WOKE BEFORE THE SUN HAD
cleared the mountains, the window filled with a soft
grey light. Fragment dreams still haunted the edges of his mind. He rose and looked over the town. A
slight mist hugged the streets. The sounds of roosters
and distant timber trucks. He showered in the common bathroom and when he was dressed, he packed all
of his belongings into the suitcase and duffel. Coming
down the stairs, he found Deedee crossing the lobby
toward the reception desk. She cocked her head and
lifted an eyebrow.

"Thought you was stayin' another night at least,"
she said. "Hope this ain't about what happened with
the tramp."

"No, ma'am. I have some business up near the Tennessee line."

She wouldn't stop looking at him funny.

"Ain't much along the Tennessee line unless you're
headed to Mountain City. You goin' through Green
Valley or takin' the Payne Gap?"

"Well, I suppose that's up to my guide."

"Guide?"

"Just a local guide I hired on."

She nodded suspiciously.

"Well, then. However you go, be careful of moonshiners. Plenty of stills up there to this day. They drive like regular speed demons on those mountain roads. Send you straight into a ditch if you're not careful."

"I'll keep that in mind."

"I'm not foolin', Charlie. Couple years back we had a schoolteacher go missin' up thataway. Headed to Mountain City on the Tennessee side. She was out of work and lookin' to take over a class up there. This was in the springtime. It wasn't till October they found her car upside down in a grove of poplar trees. Bones picked clean by critters. Poor girl. They say it was moonshiners run her off the road, but you can never know for certain."

"That must have been hard on the children."

"What children?"

"You said she was a schoolteacher."

"I said she was out of work. You need to pay attention when people speak."

Charlie resisted the urge to roll his eyes. Instead, he handed her the room key and they walked through the lobby to the corner of the street where they said goodbye. He was halfway across the street when she called to him again.

"I forgot to give you a message," she said. "A woman named Barbara called while you were in the shower. Nice lady. She said to call as soon as you can."

He thanked her with a polite wave and continued across the road.

He locked his suitcase in the cab of the pickup and slung the duffel over his shoulder, then walked the three short blocks to Mac's for a quick breakfast and a cup of coffee. It was just before eight o'clock and there were three other men at the counter eating and casually sipping from ceramic mugs. An elderly couple sat in a booth at the back of the diner bickering over what kind of weather the day was likely to produce. The woman wore a linen blindfold over her eyes and her hair was white as salt.

Mac sidled from the kitchen door to assess the diners at the counter. He wore a white shirt and hat and a red-striped tie that tucked into a white apron with lateral streaks of dish grease at the belly. He regarded Charlie with a nod and a quick flash of his index finger to let him know it would be a minute. When he came back out, he pointed his chin at the duffel and smiled.

"Headed out of town already, Charlie?" He spoke with a deep, guttural voice like a truck climbing a country road in low gear. "With those shiners you got, can't say I really blame you."

"Not quite yet," said Charlie. He settled onto the stool and studied the letterboard menu behind the counter. "I got word of a little village up north. Thought I'd check it out before leaving town tomorrow."

"That so? What's it called?"

"Wyldton. Heard of it?"

Mac shook his head. "Lots of little places up that way, tucked away in the sticks. Never heard of Wyldton, though." He turned to the other three at the counter. "Any of you old broads hear of a little village called Wyldton?"

The three men looked up from their newspapers and shook their heads.

"How'd you hear of it?" asked Mac.

"The folks at the Gambit told me about it. You know that little dive bar down the street?"

"In that case, you're likely headed to some old moonshiner's camp. I'd stay on my toes if you know what I mean."

"They seem all right to me."

Mac shrugged.

"Well, it ain't for me to say. You can take care of yourself, so I've heard. Least I could do is send you off with a full stomach."

Charlie was halfway through giving his order when the elderly woman rose from the booth with her palms scanning the room as if they were surrogate eyes. Her husband was trying to get her to sit back down, but she ignored him.

"Mac?" she called. "Are you there?"

"I'm here, Rinny," said Mac.

She stood in the center of the room with her root-like fingers splayed over the linen blindfold.

"Mac, were you askin' about a little village called Wyldton?"

Everyone in the room was watching her.

"Yes, ma'am," said Mac.

"When I was in grade school there was a little boy who joined my class halfway through the school year. Just a little ragdoll with bones like willow wands. Such a delicate boy. He didn't speak, the poor child. We thought he was perfectly mute. We only know'd his name was Oswyn and he wore the most peculiar clothes."

"Sit down, Rinny," said her husband. "They don't care."

"Let her talk, Hal," said Mac.

She continued in a wizened, meandering cadence.

"Some days he would bring a little apple doll to class. Two apple dolls, in fact. Heavens, them doll faces were hideous. Just rotten. But they wore the most darlin' little jumpers with ringin' bells along the front and lace hems. The boy was picked on, you know. When you're that odd it just can't be helped, I suppose. One day, we found him down in the creek behind the schoolhouse, three boys tryin' to clobber him good. The poor child. He was yellin' at 'em in a funny accent. He sounded like a little limey. Said he was goin' to miss supper and his mum would be cross. Wouldn't you believe it? Mac, you listenin' to any of this?"

"I'm listenin', Rinny."

"Well, it was the first time we'd heard him speak. He ran off cryin' and when we finally caught up to him, he was just settin' there with his dolls in his lap sayin' how he wanted to run back home to Wyldton. Said it was a village way up where the fir trees grow and the black bears roam, where they made apple dolls for the children, and everybody treated him kindly. Heck, the way he told it, I hoped he'd take me with him." She turned and patted the booth with her fingertips and Hal helped her into the seat. She sat quietly with her head down as if in prayer. There were tears weeping from beneath the blindfold, tracking down the deep grooves of her face. "Oh, little Oswyn, I wonder what became of you," she whispered. "Too meek for this world, perhaps."

When he reached the drug store it was eight-thirty, and the door was locked. A sign in the window read HELL IS REAL. He jiggled the door. He let a few minutes pass and then he knocked loudly and rapped on

the glass. He circled the building and found a rear
door with a chain and padlock, and he knocked there,
too. He pounded hard with the heel of his palm, calling for Halbert.

A woman strolling past with a small dog on a leash
stopped and watched him. She wore a long plaid dress
and a pearl-colored headscarf.

"You lookin' for Mr. Halbert?"

Charlie removed his hat and held it at his navel.

"Yes, ma'am."

"Saw him not long ago drivin' out to Wagoner to
see his cousin."

"How long is he usually gone?"

She shielded her face with her hand as if divulging
some dark secret.

"He don't keep regular hours, to be frank. Spends
most of his time on the river doin' the Lord's work. If
you're lookin' for a prescription, I'd consider a drive
down to Wilkesboro instead. You didn't hear it from
me."

"How long would that take?"

"Less than an hour by car, I'd reckon. Catch a mati-
nee while you're at it. That's what I'd do. I hear there's
a new Abbott and Costello with Boris Karloff and you
know that's got to be good."

Charlie thanked her and circled to the front of the
store where he jiggled the handle with hostility. He
stared contemptuously at the HELL IS REAL sign
and shook his head.

"Goddamn holy rollers," he muttered.

He went back down Main Street and stepped into
the phone booth on the corner, and with a handful of
change from breakfast, he placed a call to Washington. Barb picked up after the second ring.

"Barb, it's me, Charlie."

"Oh, Charlie. I was hoping it was you. Why haven't you been calling?

"I'm sorry. I've been so busy down here."

"I hope so. Hostetter isn't very happy with you at the moment."

"Is he there? I'll straighten it out."

"He's in a meeting. But he gave me another message to read. Do you want me to read it to you now?"

"Do I have a choice?"

Barb offered a nervous laugh.

"He told me to read it when you called. I suppose you could hang up and I could just pretend you heard it."

"It's okay. Go ahead, Barb."

"Just to prepare you, it's a sternly-worded note."

"I can handle it."

"He says: 'Mr. Danwitter, your lack of progress in the Blue Ridge Zone is disappointing. As the only inspector on special assignment now, we had high expectations for your activities. Unfortunately, we found your only correspondence received thus far to be lacking in detail and context. Please note there will be a Cabinet meeting on October 12th. If we do not receive adequate field reports from you, please prepare for immediate reassignment and disciplinary review.'" Barb took a breath. "That's all it says. No sign-off or anything. I hope it doesn't sting too much, Charlie."

"Barb, please pass along a message for me."

"I'm listening."

"Tell him I've got something good. Expect full documentation, including 8 mm reel, several rolls of 35 mm film, full-color prints, soil samples, and extensive field notes. I'm attending a harvest festival today and everything is lined up for me. I expect complete local support. That means cultural context as well. Tell Hostetter I will personally deliver everything first thing Monday morning. I expect him to be quite impressed."

"What variety are you working on?"

"They call it a 'Red Squire'."

"I got it. He'll be happy to hear it. I overheard Brannan reading him the riot act yesterday and I think he's just taking everything out on you."

"It's all water under the bridge. Come Monday, we'll start putting together a presentation for the Cabinet meeting. It will knock his socks off."

"And you're safe, Charlie?"

"Yes, I'm fine. I heard about Gibbets. You don't have to keep it a secret."

"Well, that's why I'm asking of course. They recovered his film reel. Can you believe it? They sent a team from DOJ to shake down the locals. Some real no-nonsense fellas. They tracked his equipment to a pawn shop in Charleston."

"Did you watch it?"

"I saw it all." Her voice quavered. "Hostetter screened it yesterday afternoon in a closed meeting and they had me operate the projector. It was horrifying, Charlie. It all happened while he was filming. I just can't get it out of my mind. Such violence. When you went quiet, well I feared the worst."

"Don't worry about me. I couldn't be better."

"Oh, I'm so glad to hear it. Then I'll see you Monday?"

"Yes, ma'am. And Barb?"

"Yes, Charlie?"

"Is Hostetter really in a meeting?"

"Well, no," she whispered. "He came in half-drunk and went straight to sleep on the sofa. As bad as he looked, he might still be out when you get back."

———————

Cal wore a yellow floral dress with a cinched waist and a white silk bow in her hair. She flashed Charlie a playful smile as he helped her into the cab of the pickup. Bright, grey-blue eyes like polished river stones. Still, he couldn't help notice the dark lines that appeared at her eyecorners when she glanced out the windshield, something strange and sad that betrayed her carefree aura. When they were just a mile up the road, she removed a nickel-plated flask from a small handbag and took a long drink. She shook the flask and offered it to Charlie.

"Care for a nip?" she asked.

"Depends," said Charlie. "What's the drink special?"

"Ain't never been a drop of booze in this thing that wasn't whiskey."

"In that case, pass it on over."

She lit a cigarette from the push lighter in the dash and cranked down the window an inch or two. The cool air whipsawed the tobacco smoke around the cab of the truck. Her smile widened whenever he glanced over, a small dimple on her left cheek like the calyx of a fruit.

"You keep smiling like that and I'll miss the next curve in the road," said Charlie.

"At least we'll die smilin'."

They went through Warrensville and up Highway 88, along the elusive north fork of the New River that came and went just beyond the shoulder of the road.

Forested hills rioted in fiery colors on either side of the highway. Every so often the trees would thin, and some distant mountain peak would loom briefly over the landscape before the dense tree canopies swallowed it up again.

"Sheriff Danaver told me your name was Calypso," said Charlie.

"That right?"

"Is he wrong?"

"No, he ain't wrong. Just has a bad habit of slanderin' my name all over town."

"It wasn't like that. He was asking me about the robbery and wanted to know where I was that night. He asked about the bar."

"I know he looks professional, but he ain't. Trust me. You don't know the half about ol' Dave Danaver."

He flicked the radio knob and searched for a clear station. "Are your parents music fans?"

"My parents are dead, Charlie."

"I'm sorry."

"Ain't your fault. But that's how my brother and I come to run the bar. They liked music well enough, though. Enough to spend a fortune on a fancy jukebox just before they passed on. Why do you ask?"

"Because of your name. I thought maybe they liked Calypso music."

She laughed.

"You kiddin' me? If the record didn't have a six-string and a cowboy hat on the cover, my folks wouldn't touch it with a ten-foot pole."

"Sounds like we have more in common than we thought."

"Your parents like country music, too?"

"No, the other thing."

She gave a confused look, then: "Oh, I'm sorry."

He smiled politely.

"Ain't your fault."

Charlie spun the radio dial as far as it would go and was working his way back when Cal screamed for him to look out. He jumped on the brake pedal with both feet. The rear tires squealed and fishtailed over the highway and the truck came to a stop crosswise in the road in a cloud of white smoke.

"You all right?" he asked.

Cal nodded, bracing herself against the dashboard. She pulled the door latch and stepped onto the road.

A green Dodge pickup sat partway in the shoulder, the engine compartment crudely folded around a thick maple tree. An enormous buck lay pitched on its side, straddling the lanes with a glassy black eye tilted at the tree canopy. A rear leg pumped tracklessly in the air. Charlie skirted the animal and approached the pickup. A figure lay slumped over the steering wheel—a half-bald man in his late thirties with flecks of grey in his beard. The sheet metal groaned when Charlie pulled the door open. He studied the man for signs of life.

At closer look, there was no life to assess.

Blood lacquered the dash and the windshield glass. The impact looked to have cracked his skull partly open. A grey substance fouled the bushy hair by his ears and some of it was sagging down the curvature of the steering wheel.

"Charlie, over there." Cal pointed down the road with one hand covering her mouth.

A woman lay twenty feet beyond the wreckage, a tangle of brown hair and tattered dress fabric. Charlie ran to her and kneeled on the asphalt. Her eyelids fluttered. She stared out beyond the tree canopy, blue eyes searching. Her face was white as a sheet and full of old pockmark scars.

"Can you hear me, ma'am?" said Charlie.

Her eyes stopped searching and suddenly trained on his voice.

"Are we dead?" she asked. She was bleeding from the shoulder and her front teeth looked broken. Her speech was sloppy and difficult to understand.

"No, ma'am. You were in an accident. Can you move?"

She shut her eyes and took a long shuddering breath. When she opened them again, she was staring right at him.

"You got a dead man's voice," she said. "Don't hear no life a-tol."

"Ma'am, we're going to get help, okay?"

"Ain't you even alive?" she asked.

"Yes, ma'am. Charlie Danwitter's my name. I'm alive and so are you."

The buck snorted and let out a sad bellow.

"Like a man readin' his own tombstone. That's how you sound to me." She mimicked the buck's wail, her hot breath vaporing the air. Moaning and snorting. It seemed to excite the dying buck and the creature bawled with her in an eerie duet.

Another truck screeched to a halt from the opposite direction and two men in overalls tumbled out of the doors.

"Mrs. Harrington," said one of the men. He was looking back and forth from the wrecked Dodge to the buck and back down to the woman in the road. He took one look into the cab of the Dodge, placed his hat on his chest, and hurried back to the woman. "Let's get you to the doctor," he told her.

"I think she's in shock," said Charlie. He felt his stomach tighten and a flutter of anxiety wash up his chest and neck. He patted his pockets instinctively for the absent bottle of Nembutal. "She's not making any sense. Brain trauma, maybe."

Neither man responded. They moved around Charlie like water past a stone, scooping the woman from beneath her arms, the other by the legs. The woman and the dying animal grunting and bawling in unison, their voices rising in a sad quaver.

"Sing me a dead man's song," she howled. "Sing it with grave roots wrung around your throat. Sing it from your rotten grave!"

They lifted her into the bed of the pickup, backed onto the shoulder, and gunned down the road in the direction they came. He could still hear her howling when they disappeared around the bend.

Charlie rose and found Cal sitting in the Ford, waiting for him. Her hands covered her face, and she was shaking her head slowly.

"That was the gruesomest thing I ever saw," she said.

Charlie wished he could say the same. He offered a rueful smile and held her hand for a moment, then he fired the ignition and weaved the pickup carefully around the buck. When they were a couple of miles down the road, he asked for Cal's flask and took a pull. She took it back and drank deeply.

"What was she screamin' about?" said Cal.

"Just nonsense. The crash rattled her good."

"I'd say it rattled the other guy worse."

She opened her bag and pulled out two five dollar bills.

"Found some money in his wallet. Let's pick up some more whiskey in the next town up the highway."

"You stole his wallet?"

"No, I just took the cash out of it. He won't need it."

Charlie shook his head.

"Don't look so disappointed, Charlie."

He looked her over, trying to make sense of what she'd done.

"Forget it. I just didn't expect it."

"I didn't expect to see a man's brains all over the goddamn place. Least he could do is buy me a drink and a pack of smokes. Look how my goddamn hands are tremblin'."

"I've seen worse than that and I didn't rob anyone."

"Like I said, he don't need it."

"Maybe he has kids. They could have used the cash."

"Ten dollars?"

"It'll spend at the department store, won't it?"

She folded her arms.

"Now you're makin' me feel bad about it."

"I said forget it. Doesn't matter anymore."

"Seems like it matters to you."

They drove the next few miles in silence. When they came to the small town of Fig, Cal motioned out the window and told him to pull over. They sat idling for a moment outside a primitive general store until Cal slipped the two fives from her handbag and handed one to Charlie.

"Tell you what," she said. "I'm gonna buy a decent bottle of whiskey and a box of cookies for the road. Why don't you put the other five in the mailbox of that sad little hillbilly church across the street. We'll split the difference."

"I still don't think it shakes out."

"Why not?"

"Because I didn't take the money from the dead guy, you did."

"So you want me to buy the booze and give the rest to the church?"

"The church was your idea. I'm not a churchgoer."

"Then, what? You just want to leer while I stroll across the street with the wind blowin' my dress up?"

He grinned.

"I could think of worse things."

She slapped his thigh and emptied the rest of the whiskey down her throat. "Goddamn. I can't tell if I'm gettin' involved with a pope or a pervert."

"If I had a nickel every time somebody told me that."

She disappeared into the general store and when she returned, she was carrying a fresh bottle in a paper bag, a pack of cigarettes, and a box of Crispo chocolate chip cookies. She set everything on the front seat and gave Charlie a raised eyebrow and told him to stay put. She crossed the street with the mountain wind stirring her hair and bright yellow dress and she went to the mailbox in front of the run-down church and flipped open the little wooden door. The church could have passed for an abandoned building if it wasn't for the freshly mowed lawn and Bible verses bannered over the front porch. A thick rind of moss clung to the wooden eves. She set the five dollar bill inside the church mailbox, gave a quick look up and down the street, and then she hiked her dress up past her hips. She shook her ass back and forth at Charlie and went back to the passenger door and climbed in.

"What was that for?" said Charlie, with a laugh.

"Figured I'd try to please a pope and a pervert in one shot."

The river forked past the town of Fig, and they followed the northern tributary along a road that had not been paved in decades. Charlie wheeled the truck around potholes and the stony washes that had swept much of the old macadam into the creek. The late-morning sun passed behind islands of cumulus. None of the trees had gone barren and they still held plenty of color. Black willows shot cantilevered branches over the water. Buckeye and hickory on the hillsides.

"Been meanin' to tell you," said Cal. She opened her bag and slipped a small gold ring onto her ring finger. "We'll have to be married."

"What, now?"

"You heard me. Married. Man and wife."

"You're not even going to propose?" he said, feigning shock.

"I propose you do what I say unless you want to sleep alone tonight."

He was still playing it up.

"I think we're moving a little fast, dear. You haven't even met Mama."

"Shush up. It's just pretend. They'll split us up otherwise."

"We'll have to get our stories straight. Where did we spend our honeymoon?"

She thought on it with a long, ponderous hum.

"What if we're on our honeymoon now? We just got married, and we're passin' through on our way to Nashville for the Grand Ole Opry. I've always dreamed of goin' to Nashville, Charlie."

"Works for me, dear."

They passed a large black barn that was missing much of its lumber. The faint letterings of the word FRUIT painted on the side.

"I recognize that barn," said Cal. She'd been sipping off the fresh whiskey bottle and her speech was beginning to sound sloppy. "There's a fruit stand just around the bend. We used to stop there on the way up."

"Want me to stop?"

"Reckon you'd appreciate it. If I remember it right, there were all sorts of apples and other fruit for sale. Maybe you can talk shop while we're there. And I've got to use the commode."

They pulled onto a dirt road with an old faded market sign and went through a stand of buckeyes into a sunny clearing. The area was deserted. Old merchant stands lay collapsed on either side of the road, overturned field wagons rotting in the dead grass. Brambles of creeper vines twisted through the ruins. It looked like the site of some long-ago massacre.

"I wonder where they all went?" said Cal. "Used to be a dozen farmers this time of year. Candied apples and sweet cider. They even had a little pettin' zoo with goats and rabbits. We'd stay for hours."

"Times sure are changing," said Charlie. "Looks like they left years ago."

At the end of the row sat a stone hut with a canvas tarpaulin roof. A sheet of woodsmoke drifted across the clearing. Circling the hut stood little stone pedestals with domed wicker baskets placed upside down atop the stands. As Charlie idled the truck, a honeybee appeared on the windshield, pockets full of orange pollen like tiny saddlebags. It made a small circle on the glass and flew out toward the stone hut.

"It's an apiary," said Charlie. He had his hand on the door lever and was about to climb out when Cal grabbed his hand.

"You think somebody lives here?" she said.

"Sure I do. He's right over there."

A figure came shambling from the hut with a large denim hood and a circular wicker faceguard. The hood was fastened to the wicker plate so it looked like the head of a large hammer. He stood watching the truck between the weaves of his mask for a moment before lifting the hood from his shoulders. Beneath was an old man with a long beard and sagging overalls. He swapped the hood for a straw hat and pulled thoughtfully at the vee of his beard.

Charlie stepped out of the truck and stood at the front bumper.

"Hidy," the man called.

"Hello," said Charlie. "We're just passing through. The missus says this used to be a farm stand."

The skepper hobbled with an arthritic gait. Insects circled in a thick swarm as he approached.

"You have to repeat yourself. I can't hear much a-toll."

"The farm stand," said Charlie. "I'm curious what happened to it."

Cal had come out of the truck and stood at Charlie's side.

"They shut down when the war ended," said the skepper.

Charlie glanced about at the ruins.

"Which war?"

The old man laughed.

"Well, it weren't the one with Lincoln if that's what you was gettin' at."

"Pershing, then?"

"You're gettin' warm."

Cal let out a loud shriek. A pair of honeybees were inspecting the floral patterns of her dress. Antennae twitching with that strange and frenetic sentience. She gave them each a gentle flick and looked about warily at the swarm.

"If it's not any trouble we'd like to use your john," said Charlie. "I'd pay you for it."

"John?" said the skepper.

"You know, the ladies."

"I got a shitter in back if it's what you needed."

Charlie glanced at Cal with a smirk.

"A shitter will do."

The old man waved his arms like he'd just recalled something important.

"The queen," he said. He opened the pocket of his overalls and produced a tiny woven ball about the size of a walnut. "Got distracted and forgot all about her. No wonder they's makin' a fuss." He held the wicker ball to the sky and inspected it with squinted eyes. An angry sound like an electric current inside. "Hear that? She don't like the sunshine. Go ahead around back, miss. I'll put this here queenie where she wants to be."

"I could wait," she said.

Charlie gave another wry smile. "At this point, I think it'd be rude."

She gave him a dirty look and went around the back of the stone hut, swatting the air as she went. The old man unhooked a bee skep from a nearby hickory tree and set it on an empty pedestal. He tilted it slightly and placed the wicker ball underneath the lip and he gazed into the sky as if he could read divinations in the angles of bees.

"Sorry for the trouble," said Charlie.

"Shit. Ain't no trouble. Used to be hunerds of folks come through here. Good money to be made back then. Seemed like every day was worth gettin' up for. Best part was when the farmers would pack up for the day and the hooch would get to flowin'. Good homemade hooch made with birch syrup and none of that bonded government piss. That shit'll take the hair off a wooden leg, let me tell you. We'd spend all the money we made gamblin' and drinkin'. Once or twice a year they'd bring a couple girls from the city and things would get strange. Not for me, though. Never took to whorin'. Brother, it was all them poor drunk farmers could do to get back home in one piece."

"What happened to them all?"

"Who's that?"

"Where did they go?"

"Lots of folks is sellin' their farms. Sometimes the kids inherit a farm and don't want nothin' to do with it. Some get tangled up with the banks and can't get themselves untangled. Can't stand a banker. You ain't one, are you?"

"No, sir."

"What now?"

"I said no."

"My friend Ed Little sold his apple orchard to a golf course company. There ain't nothin' but grass, now. You can see it from the highway. Highway 88, that is. Ed made himself enough to quit workin' though. Them golf folks paid me good money to haul out a hive from a willow tree. That was two years ago. Tell you what, I'd take a big, beautiful orchard over a bunch

of bullshit grass any ol' time. Might as well be a goddamn desert, but that's one man's opinion. If there's
a miracle left to be had, maybe there's somethin' still
alive way down deep where those treeroots once lived.
Somethin' twistin' slow and easy through all that
High Country clay. Maybe it remembers what it was
like to be an apple tree and it's just a-waitin' for this
wretched age of man to end 'fore it comes sproutin'
back."

Charlie opened the door and brought out the bottle
of whiskey and offered it to the skepper. He drank ea-
gerly and wiped his hairy mouth with the back of his
hand. Cal came from around the hut and pressed in
close to Charlie. They passed the bottle around until
the skepper declined.

"That's all I can handle till the sun goes down," he
said. "Them bees don't like a drunk. Makes 'em ornery
and nobody wants an ornery bee."

"How much for your bee skeps?" asked Charlie.

"Do what?"

"Your skeps. How much could I pay you for one?"

"Three dollars is what I'm askin'."

He handed over the money and the old man unhooked another one from the side of the hut. Charlie
looked it over admiringly.

"Get yourself a queen as pretty as the lady on your
arm and you'll have plenty of sweet honey," said the
skepper.

"I thought you could only have one queen at a time,"
said Charlie.

"What now?"

"One queen at a time."

"Well, depends on what kind of sting your alpha
queen's got. The lady with the deadliest sting wins."

They both looked at Cal.

She cracked a smile and took a drunken step backward with her middle finger held aloft. "How's this for a deadly sting?"

The old man snorted. "Reckon I been stung thataway more'n any other."

As they neared the Tennessee line, the big, forested peaks they'd seen from the highway shrank to flinty outcroppings and scree slopes. They were skirting the summit now. The sky grew big, dark conifers taking the place of the big-leafed trees. They pulled off the road, and by early afternoon they came to a dirt crossing in the center of a highland meadow. It looked as if nobody had come through in many weeks. Late-season weeds flowered between the old tire marks in the rut road. Cal stepped out of the truck and turned a slow circle in the crossroads with her arms outstretched and her index finger pointing out the cardinal directions. Charlie watched, grinning from behind the wheel.

"You figure it out, dear?" he shouted.

"Reckon it's thataway." She had one hand over her eyes as if navigating by psychic ability alone. "Definitely gettin' somethin' from this direction."

"That ain't even a road."

She threw her hands in the air.

"I don't know. Been a long time."

Charlie exited the truck and looked about. The field grass was still wet with dew. The mountain fog must have burned off just moments ago. Fir tree groves lay in all directions. He could smell the astringency of conifers and the weediness of the meadow. He lit two cigarettes and handed her one. The wind shifted directions and picked up the tobacco smoke and blew it south. When he turned to the northern edge of the clearing, he could hear the faint bleating of goats.

"You hear that?" said Charlie.

"It's my stomach. Whiskey and cookies ain't the best road food."

"Not that. Listen."

They stood silently, ears tilted. The white noise of mountain wind. Crows chanting.

And there it was again.

"Goats?"

"That's what I thought."

From the trees, a herd of goats bounded into the meadow with their strange chortling calls and the clanging of nannybells. There might have been a dozen, maybe more. A sheepdog ran beside, nipping their hooves and dodging the horns that would sometimes rear up. Coming up behind the herd was a small man with a red wool shawl wrapped over one shoulder and a wool cap pulled low over his brows. He walked briskly, stabbing at the ground with a long staff decorated with a horned skull. The sound of the herd intensified as they drew near. Charlie had to shout over them to address the goat herder.

"Sir? Excuse me," he called.

The man stopped and regarded them with a suspicious tilt of the head. A grey and white beard hung from his diminutive face in two long spears. A tiny merlin of the woods.

"Sir, do you know the town of Wyldton?"

The man nodded mutely and swung his staff in a slow arc, the goats scampering from its reach. He placed the walking end of the staff into the soft dirt and drew a line. He finished it with two slanted marks to form a westward-pointing arrow.

Charlie and Cal looked that way.

"How far?" asked Charlie.

He held out his hand and measured an inch between his fingers.

"Thank you," Cal said loudly, as if he might be hard of hearing, too.

A brown and white goat with large testicles leapt onto the front bumper of the truck, rattling its horns against the grill. The goat herder clicked his teeth and the sheepdog bullied it off the truck and back into the fray. He tipped his head and touched his brow in a parting gesture and continued down the path.

Charlie helped Cal into the truck and they continued west until the rut road was joined by a fast-running stream that wound along the road's shoulder. The stream continued, but the road went up a steep grade and ended at a dusty cul-de-sac with a half-dozen old cars and trucks parked in a semicircle.

"I remember now," said Cal. "There's a little trail through the trees and then it's right there. A ten-minute walk if I remember it right. We made it, Charlie."

He untied the luggage from the truck bed and they started down the trail. The path was muddy and crowded with roots and stones. Soon, flagstones fanned out around them in alternating patterns of dark and light, some scrawled with crude drawings of trees with tiny faces peering from the hollows of the trunks. When they finally broke through the treeline, they stood before a tiny mountain village surrounded by fir trees. The buildings were constructed of dark hardwood with sloping A-frame roofs, the largest of which was a church with a bronze bell. In the center of the village stood a large apple orchard of about a hundred trees of varying age and size. The branches held much fruit, and no fallen apples could be seen on the ground. The trees looked older at the far end, progressing to younger trees and saplings up front. A reed flute played in some corner of the village and there were several men laying a large bonfire at the near end of the orchard with freshly split logs. Hens foraged between the tree trunks. One of the men spotted them and came walking over wearing a wool tunic, dark trousers tucked into his boots. Long dark hair pulled back. He had a friendly smile and walked with his hands resting on his hips.

"Hello," said the man. "Are ye lost or did ye come for the celebration?" The accent was strange, every bit hillfolk drawl but with a curious British patois. "We get a mix of both comin' through this way."

Cal stepped forward with a big smile.

"That you, Gwilym?"

He gave her a polite, but ponderous look.

"That is my name, yes."

"It's me, Cal. Calypso Buchanan. Well, it's Danwitter now."

His expression brightened.

"Yes, of course. Beech's sister. It's been so long."

"I ain't just my brother's sister, you know," she said, playfully.

"Of course. Where are my manners? Welcome back, friend." He gave her a quick hug and looked expectantly at Charlie. "Who's your guest?"

"This is my husband, Charlie Danwitter. He's really into apples."

"Well, you've certainly come at the right time, Mr. Danwitter."

"Please, call me Charlie," he said, and shook his hand.

"Will ye be stayin' the night?" asked Gwilym. "My grandad's house is empty on account of his passin' in the spring. Stay there if ye wish."

"Well, that would be fine," said Charlie. "As long as it won't put you out."

"Won't put anyone out one bit."

Gwilym took their overnight bags and ushered them toward the center of the village, where others had already gathered to greet the newcomers. Many embraced Cal affectionately, while others introduced themselves for the first time. The villagers were gracious and friendly, the men all dressed similarly with wool tunics and brown trousers. Old men and young men alike.

The women wore long cotton dresses, some with a green overdress tied at the waist with leather strands. After shaking nearly thirty hands, Gwilym brought them to the far end of the village where a sturdy shack sat among others of similar size and shape. He had a large glass jug in his hands and he handed it to Charlie.

"Made fresh this mornin'. Best cider ye ever tasted, I'll bet."

Charlie looked it over.

"I have no doubt. Thank you."

"I could come back in an hour to give a quick tour."

"That would be wonderful," said Charlie.

"Don't forget to take him through the orchard," said Cal. "It'll drive him wild, and I could use a little rest besides."

"It'll be my pleasure."

Gwilym left them alone in the shack, which was just a ten-by-ten square room with a bed, a wood-stove, and a small table for an oil lamp. On the walls hung long pinewood shelves filled with old books and wooden figurines, including a set of handmade chess pieces carved from oakwood and a bust of an old woman. Charlie picked up a thorny ball woven from berry brambles and turned it over carefully in his hands. An odd assortment of items.

"Told you they was nice people," said Cal.

Charlie had taken a sip from the jug of cider and was looking over the bottle. "Impressive."

"The town or the cider?"

"Both. I didn't know what to expect, but so far, I'm astonished. I've been run off nearly every orchard in the county. Then I show up here and these folks give me a jug of cider and a place to stay. You don't know what good timing this is for me, Cal. Did you see that orchard?"

"I knew you'd love it." Cal sprawled on the bed and yawned. "Why don't you come lay down with me?"

He took off his shoes and they lay together, Cal running her hands over his shirt with her fingernails.

"Thanks for bringin' me," she said. "Somethin's been pullin' me back for years and I was tired of ignorin' it. I felt this place right over the horizon every time I looked up. Like I could see it in the mountains if I looked hard enough. Now that I'm back, I just feel so calm."

"How old is this village?"

"I don't know. How old is New York City?"

"Can't be that old. No way."

"My grandad was born here. Had to be eighteen-sixties or so. He said his grandad was born here, too. But he told a lot of tall tales about this place. I think it was mostly the hooch talkin'. They got good hooch, here. Maybe they'll bring it out tonight."

"What kind of tall tales?"

"Come on, Charlie. I'm tired."

"Just tell me one."

"Well, there was one that stuck with me. He'd say the town got started when a group of explorers went lookin' for a pass through the mountains. They came across the Cherokee and I guess all hell broke loose. Well, accordin' to him, they fought so long that winter came and they had to quit fightin' and hunker down. It was a bad winter, so they all joined up to survive down in the caves. What was left of 'em, I guess."

"And they never left?"

"That's what he said."

"Doesn't sound too crazy."

"It does to me. How do you go from killin' each other to lovin' each other just like that? Don't add up."

"When I was in the war, we fought with British troops. Not every day, but we knew they were there. We used to be enemies way back when. Sometimes it takes a newer, meaner enemy to make you befriend an old enemy."

"Who would be the new enemy in grandad's story?"

"Starvation, maybe. Could be lots of things."

"Well that's the easiest pill to swallow. There's others."

"Tell me."

"Tell you what, dear. Once that hooch gets flowin' you can ask all the questions you want. You seen how friendly they are. I'm sure they'll tell you all about it. Matter of fact, that's the likeliest explanation for this place. A couple of hillbillies came up here to make moonshine and never left. Get you a woman or two and next thing you know it's a village. If they're honest, I bet that's what they'll say. For now, I just want to lay here and close my eyes for a bit."

———————

The apple trees were pruned at exactly nine feet and trimmed to a conical shape so sunlight reached the lateral branches below. The fruit grew large and plentiful. Dark red skin almost the color of beets. Charlie wandered through the trees, marveling at the lack of pests of any kind. Strong, grey limbs slightly oranged with lichen. No weeds grew in the alleys. He pinched the soil between his fingers and brought it to his nose. A rich, mineral odor. At the center of the orchard, he found a stone pedestal carved with a contradictory assortment of glyphs. Alchemical symbols mingled with Christian iconography and indigenous petroglyphs, all wrapping the circumference of the pedestal to form the unlikeliest of psalms. As he continued, the trees grew younger, until the last row consisted of waist-high saplings staked to willow wands.

"We plant a new tree each time someone in our village dies," said Gwilym. "If ye go back far enough, you'll find trees honoring our founders. They no longer bear fruit, but the roots are alive."

"How old are they?" asked Charlie.

"Centuries."

"I've never heard of a fruit tree living that long."

Gwilym turned his palms humbly.

"Now ye have."

"Will it be all right if I take a few photographs? The folks I work with would love to see this. It's one of the most beautiful orchards I've ever seen."

"Reckon it'll be fine. But we must get permission from the Scrivener."

"The Scrivener?"

"Just a formality. Shouldn't be a problem. I'll take ye once you've gotten the lay of the land."

He led Charlie past the unlit bonfire and through the rows of benches set out in anticipation of the harvest festival. They passed the small church with its humble belfry and flower beds brimming with flowering herbs. They climbed a steep hill studded with conifers. The path wound along the back of the village and offered a clear view of all the buildings and their occupants, which Gwilym detailed with a demographer's meticulousness. The trail ended at a bluff overlooking the high country where fields of sunflowers and flax stretched over the sloping hills and wild ponies rested in the shade of the trees.

A sprawling hemlock tree grew near the bluff amid jumbles of mossy logs and knee-high grasses. Charlie abruptly stopped and gave the tree a hard stare. A corpse lay horizontally in the middle branches, wrapped in a black and white wool blanket and secured with a thick rope. A pair of ravens stood atop the corpse and croaked when the two men drew near.

"This is my grandad, Oswyn," said Gwilym. "Died in the very cabin you're stayin' in. Wish he could've seen one more harvest, but I'm happy he died here in Wyldton. He loved this village till the end."

The corpse gaped eyeless at the sky, a thin white ruff clinging to the back of the skull. Scavengers and weather had completely stripped the meat from the bone, save for a few blackened tendons around the joints. The pose was strangely artificial. Pin-like fingers intertwined in prayer. A ghastly expression of surprise.

Charlie considered the skeleton, searching for something to say about it.

"He's been up there since the spring?"

"Yessir. He passed in April."

One of the ravens grew nervous and launched from the corpse's blanket, gliding down below the bluff and out of sight. The other soon followed.

"Is everyone given this type of burial?" Charlie struggled with the last word.

"Oh yes. It's our tradition to give back to the mountains what we can."

"Why aren't there others?"

"On the night of the harvest moon, the remains are taken down and buried in the orchard. Today, Oswyn's bones will feel the sun for the last time. Soon we'll plant a sapling atop his grave and the great orchard will grow." He swept an arm over the village below. "Look yonder, Charlie. The orchard ye been admirin' is more than it seems. Ain't just the most beautiful orchard, as ye said. It's the most beautiful cemetery, too. The roots drive the bones deep into the earth where they become life again. The mountain takes on the character of the dead, and we take on the traits of the mountain. There's a power to it that must be respected."

"Then the inscriptions on the stone pedestal are—"

"Names. Epitaphs."

"How far back do they go?"

"Centuries. Like I told ye."

"There must be a hundred trees, at least."

"Aye, a hundred souls."

"You said you were happy your grandfather died here."

"Sure I am, why do ye ask?"

"I was wondering if many people left."

"We're not prisoners if that's what you're sayin'."

"That's not what I meant, no."

"Most come back, that's the thing. I did. I left for three years myself. Made it all the way to the coast. A town called New Bern. Never found the old Bern. Joined a fishin' crew and we'd sail out into the sound, sometimes all the way to the open ocean. Picture a mountain kid like me surrounded by nothin' but the bare-naked sea. Like a new and mysterious planet. Sometimes the feelin' overwhelmed me. Just when I thought I was used to it, we nearly got sunk by whales. At least we thought they was whales. Maybe sharks. Blow after blow, hard enough to knock a man off his feet. Men were cryin'. I know I was. The hull cracked and it was all we could do to keep from goin' under. I never was so scared in my life. I can't even swim."

"Is that why you came back?"

"Partly, yes. When I first left, I was baffled by the outside world. Slowly, I got used to it. But then I found the sea even more mysterious. When I finally got my sea legs, them creatures below added a new level to it still. There's just no end to it, you know? Mysteries on top of mysteries until you don't know up from sideways. Ain't it enough to drive ye mad? I feel better now that I'm back, even though it cost me my woman. One month she spent here before she got restless and asked me to drive her back down to the coast. I'm happy even so. Although sometimes I set up here at night with Grandad, staring off into all those stars, and I picture us on a spinnin' orb in a sea so big and empty nobody can make sense of it. It could make a god look small. And that old feelin' comes back again. Like we're just fallin' forever. When I hold that perspective even for a tiny moment, hoo boy. It knocks me on my arse. Some mysteries ye can't never get used to. Can't grow sea legs to stand in every strange place, can ye? Not even in the town ye was born."

"You're not the only one who feels that way."

"Ye feel it too?"

"All the time. Like you said, it's enough to drive you mad."

"How do ye cope with it? Please tell me, Charlie."

"I don't cope with it well. I don't think anyone really does. I've seen men lose their damn minds over it. And not just men—entire countries, too. If you ever figure it out, please let me know."

"I doubt I ever will."

They stood in silence for a moment, looking over the village below. People had come to arrange the benches and there were children skipping through the orchard. You could hear them singing nursery rhymes from across the way. A slight wind swept over the bluff and a pair of warblers had begun to sing from the hells of rosebay on the hillside.

"I'd love to begin photographing before the festival starts," said Charlie. "Could you show me to the Scrivener?"

Gwilym pressed his hands together under his chin and whispered a quick prayer for his grandfather, then turned to Charlie with a smile.

"Follow me."

The Scrivener's hut wasn't much larger than the others, but it boasted large, ornate windows on all four sides. A sun etching graced the front door, a dozen sword-like rays fanning out from a stoic face. Gwilym raised his hand to knock but thought twice.

"It would be wise to have a word first. Could ye give five minutes?"

"Of course," said Charlie, backing away. "I'll come back."

He wandered through the orchard and found the stone pedestal. He kneeled, reading the names and phrases inscribed there. The stone looked to have been regularly scrubbed of moss, the letters scraped clean of dirt and debris. A strange and unlikely combination of histories recorded there.

When he returned to the shack to check on Cal, he paused at the doorway. The window beside the door was adorned with alternating white and yellow asters, all plastered around the window frame with a thin piping of mud. Sitting by the door was an apple doll with little bells down the front. The dress was well-crafted, but the head was a purplish wad with beady eyes and a gaping slantwise mouth. He stepped over the doll and pushed the door open and found Cal napping peacefully on the bed. He sidled into the shack and lifted the skep he had purchased earlier in the day and slipped out the door.

When he reached the Scrivener's hut, the door had been left partly open and Gwilym was gone. Charlie knocked lightly and peered inside.

"Come now, Squire," called an old raspy voice.

The room felt small, cluttered with antique items and stacks of newsprint. Swords and rifles mounted to the walls. Apple crates filled with paper. Ancient books pressed neatly together on the shelves, some with worn leather bindings. Behind an oakwood desk sat the Scrivener, a small elderly figure with reading glasses and patchy white hair around the scalp like an antique doll. The figure had aged beyond any easy determination of gender, and no effort was made to signal one.

"I brought a gift," said Charlie, lifting the skep. "To aid pollination in the spring. Perhaps you could set it on the stone pedestal in the orchard."

"We don't place beehives there." The Scrivener studied the skep through watery blue eyes that looked almost aquatic. "But it's a good skep, woven with Phragmites, looks like. A common water reed. The water reed products hold up well in all sorts of weather." A dip in the inkbox and a quick notation. "And I hear you're married to the Buchanan girl? Please give me your full name, Squire."

"Of course. It's Charles Danwitter."

"And your sire and mother?"

"William and Elaine."

"Alive?"

"No. Neither one."

"I see tragedy in your eyes, Squire."

"You wouldn't be wrong about that."

The Scrivener nodded and noted it in the ledger.

"Fine names, nonetheless. We've had several Williams here but no Elaines. Greek origin if I'm not mistaken. Rays of light."

"Rays of light?"

"The name's meanin'. Rays of light. Ironic given the tragic figure Elayne of Ascolat. Are you familiar with it?"

"I am not."

The Scrivener gave a strained look at the bookshelf nearest Charlie, as if the tale might be found there.

"You'd do well to acquaint yourself with the Arthurian legends. What is your occupation?"

"I'm an agricultural inspector."

"And you went to university for this?"

"Yes. On the GI Bill. Graduated last year."

"A soldier?"

"Yes."

The Scrivener reached for a newspaper from a nearby pile and laid it carefully on the desk. Skeletal hands, but steady. The front page carried a photograph of an armored caravan with American troops running alongside it.

"I've only gotten this far. I'm afraid I'm ignorant of the war's endin'. I don't get as many papers as I used to."

Charlie leaned over the desk. The newspaper was a *Washington Post* Sunday edition from January 1945.

"Would you like me to tell you?"

"I'll wager the Germans lost?"

"Yes, that's correct."

"And what of this Hitler fellow?"

"Died in a hole like a rat."

"And who has replaced him?"

"Nobody. The entire German Army surrendered in May of '45. The Japanese just a few months later."

"I don't mean Germany. Against whom are the great forces of virtue now readyin' themselves? What great evil in the world must now be stopped?"

Charlie studied the Scrivener carefully. He felt he was being led somewhere. "Now the West is mostly aligned against Communism," he said.

"Yes, of course it is. And after that, somethin' else. Evil rises, good vanquishes said evil. Evil rises again. The rivers run red. The streets run red. I've lived a long life and read five thousand books or more, but it wouldn't surprise me if one day the oceans themselves turned red. Is there enough land on Earth for all the cemeteries? Perhaps that's why the Good Lord gave us such a big planet. So we could have room to bury each other in it."

"What else are we supposed to do?"

"Son, you've got to keep the Devil at your knee. Let him curl up at the end of your bed on a windy night. Feed him scraps from the table. A hungry devil is a dangerous one indeed."

"I'm not sure I follow," said Charlie.

"Ye don't follow or ye don't agree?"

"I don't agree."

"That's all right. Ain't gonna hurt my feelins."

"There's a church here, isn't there? What does the minister say about it?"

"There's a church, but not a minister. We had one, but he ran off with a girl from the village and ain't come back yet. The folks here don't need someone barkin' at 'em every Sunday, anyhow. Especially from some randy hypocrite. We're better off without him."

"In that case, I'll say that if you allow evil to grow it will grow just as big as it can. No amount of scraps will keep it happy."

"Tell me, Squire. Is a dog more liable to bite you if you feed him or if you starve him?"

"Sure, the analogy works, but—"

"'Course it does. I read about a man in West Virginia who fell steppin' out of the bathtub. This was quite a few years ago. Must have been a bad fall 'cause he broke his back. He lay there callin' for help for three days and guess who finally came struttin' in? The damn dog. His loyal companion chewed his face clean off. Why? He was hungry, that's why. You got to keep the Devil fed, Squire. Just enough so he don't chew your face off."

"Well, I thank you for the discussion," said Charlie. He caught himself wringing his hands and he let them drop to his sides. "I did have a request, if you'd be so kind."

"Go ahead."

"I'd like to photograph the orchard out front. Maybe take some measurements. A soil sample if I could."

"Well, of course, Squire. It's your occupation to do so, is it not?"

"It is, thank you."

"Just one condition."

"What's that?"

"Daylight hours only. Once the sun goes down, put your camera in a poke and forget all about it. I can't have ye sneakin' under good folks' windows with a camera in your hand. They won't have it. Do we have an agreement?"

"Yes, absolutely. I understand."

There came a small cough from the corner of the room and Charlie spun toward the sound. A girl about the age of ten sat in a chair beneath a large Elizabethan banner embellished with golden lions and fleurs-de-lis. Her hand covered her mouth, eyes large and alert. She must have been there the whole time.

"I'm sorry," she said, her hand muffling her voice.

"Don't mind Margaret," said the Scrivener. "She watches everythin' I do and say. The smartest child in the village. She's goin' to take over my duties when I die, which shouldn't be too long now."

"Then into the tree you go," said Margaret.

"Soon enough, my girl," said the Scrivener.

———

"Get what you need, dear?" Cal had changed into a light blue dress and was sitting up in bed with the apple doll in her lap. The thing looked as if it were howling—a vicious, jangling fiend.

"I got the consent I needed," said Charlie. "This could save my entire career."

"You're welcome."

He took the doll, placed it on a shelf beside Oswyn's collection of wooden figurines, and sat beside her on the bed.

"Thank you," he said. "I mean it, really."

He kissed her neck a long time. The crook of her jaw, her delicate earlobes. She kissed him back and unbuttoned his shirt. He began to work the hem of her dress up over her knees.

"I knew that old orchard would stir you up," she said.

"You should give yourself more credit than that."

She gently stayed his hand.

"What if someone comes by?"

"Let them watch if they want."

"Charlie."

"Everybody's busy with the festival, is what I meant."

She glanced out the window and raised an eyebrow.

"It is our fake honeymoon, after all." At the foot of the bed was a large blanket knitted with black and white chevrons. She shook it out and lay beneath it with her head on the pillow. She lifted one corner of the blanket invitingly. "You gonna take off your shoes, at least?"

She was on top of him when the shack began to quake. It sounded like the whole village was outside, rapping and pounding on the wood siding. A jarring, thunderous sound. They sat up nude with the blanket shawled around them. Nobody at the windows that they could see, nobody at the door. Some of the chess pieces tumbled from the shelf and skidded across the floor. Then the apple doll. They held each other as if riding out an earthquake.

All at once, it stopped.

A child's voice began to chant a nursery rhyme, and other voices quickly joined in. As they sang, they circled the shack, dragging sticks along the old wooden boards. Charlie watched the tops of their heads barely clearing the window as they passed by. He listened to the scuffs of their feet in the dirt as they sang.

"What are they singing?" asked Charlie.

"Hell if I know," said Cal. "Never heard this one before."

They listened carefully until they made out the words.

The Chessman plays upon the board,
the Bard upon the lute,
The Harvest Queen will please the Lord
And bear the Maiden fruit.

Charlie rose from the bed and slipped into his trousers. When he opened the door, the children went skipping toward the center of town and into the orchard, some of them still chanting the nursery rhyme.

"What the hell got into them?" said Charlie.

Cal straightened her dress.

"They've been givin' those little monsters sweet cider all day, I bet. Turned 'em into a bunch of maniacs."

"You never heard that nursery rhyme?"

"Never."

"I just wonder what it meant."

"Look at you, Charlie. You seem frightened."

"Not frightened, just curious. The maiden fruit could mean all sorts of things. Fruit born from a harvest queen makes it almost seem like an actual birth. Or maybe the harvest queen is the name of a certain tree in the orchard?"

"Well, they do have a harvest queen. That part makes sense to me. She wears a pretty white dress with flowers in her hair. I always wanted to be a harvest queen but never had the chance. You'll see her when we head out there."

Charlie set the figurines back on the shelf. He picked up the apple doll and looked it over with squinted eyes. He set it next to the thorny nest and went to his camera bag, thumbed the aperture down low.

"Do me a favor and hold the door for me. I need a little extra light."

Cal went to the door and nudged it open with her hip.

"I thought the men were supposed to hold the door."

He glassed the doll with the camera lens and clicked a few frames. He stepped closer, honing the focus on that abomination of a face. He suddenly stopped and took a step back. He thought he saw the jaw working slowly in the dark folds of the putrid apple face. Like it had some dark secret it was about to tell.

"What's wrong?" asked Cal.

114 | C.W. BLACKWELL

He handed her the doll.

"You see anything strange here?"

"You got to be more specific."

"Look closely at the face."

She looked, cocked her head slightly. Her eyes widened, and she shoved it back at Charlie. "The mouth is movin'. What the hell, Charlie?"

"I thought I was crazy."

"Get that fuckin' thing out."

He walked the doll outside and held it to the light. A small blister welled up between its lips. It pulsed and grew and began to split apart. The larva of a codling moth came wagging from the doll's mouth. A creamy white tongue lapping the air. He took the larva by the head and pinched. A pink mucus stained his fingers. He wiped them on the fabric of the doll's dress and twisted the rotten apple off the body and chucked it as far as he could throw it. He stood looking at the headless doll for a moment and then he flung that out, too.

"Did you get rid of it?" said Cal. She was looking at his hands to make sure they were empty.

"Yes ma'am."

"What the hell was it?"

"It talked to me."

"What?"

He sat on the bed and pulled the blanket back.

"It said to me in a tiny little whisper: get back in bed with that pretty blonde."

She punched him playfully.

"I knew you was a dirty ol' skunk."

He entered the cool of the orchard with a fresh roll of 8 mm film whirling in the gears. A slight wind had swept up the mountain, heavy fruit bobbing on the branches. He walked slowly, camera steady, toward the older trees that no longer bore fruit. Backwards through untold seasons and atop centuries of bones. The final row stood grey and lifeless. Glyphs etched into the old bark, stretched with the passage of time. He remembered what Gwilym had said, how the roots still lived somewhere deep below the soil. Perhaps his certainty was only a matter of faith.

The church bell tolled. Charlie wandered back through the orchard to the great fire ring. They had arranged the benches in a half circle beneath the shade of the fir trees, rising gradually in height toward the back like a small stadium. A few of the villagers were sitting, listening to the lingering tones of the old bronze bell. Faces filtered out from the trees and from their shacks. Children skipped with apple dolls jangling in their hands.

He found Cal sitting at the end of the middle row, watching him. She smiled into the camera as he circled her, primping her hair like some Hollywood starlet. When he sat beside her, a young woman with a white dress and flowers in her hair strode quickly toward them. She threw her arms around Cal with tears in her eyes. Cal patted her back, threw a surprised look at Charlie.

"I'm just so happy you're here," said the woman. She was crying, but also laughing at herself at the same time. A complicated mix of emotions. "Don't ye remember me?"

Cal studied the woman. She was pretty, with long blond hair and a tiny mole on her left cheek. Light green eyes. No more than twenty years old.

"I'm sorry," she said. "I'd remember a striking thing like you."

"It's been a long time," she admitted. She wiped the tears from her cheeks and more tears followed. She took Cal's hands in hers. "But I remember ye. And I'm just so tickled to see ye. And that gorgeous dress, my goodness. Welcome, Miss Buchanan."

"Well, thank you." Cal offered a tenuous smile. "I'm not used to getting such a welcome when I turn up somewhere. What is your name?"

"I'm Abigail. It's okay if ye don't remember. Would ye like to wear my crown?" She lifted the crown of white asters and held it in the space between them, but Cal declined.

"It looks better on you, honey."

"I don't mind. Wouldn't it look fetchin' over that beautiful blue dress?"

"No, really. I insist you wear it. Ain't you the Harvest Queen?"

Abigail nodded stoically. She placed the crown back on her head and gave Cal another tight hug. She glanced at Charlie.

"Is this your husband?"

Charlie rose and offered his hand.

"Charlie Danwitter, miss. Pleasure."

"Pleasure," she replied. The hand that tugged at him was cool and delicate. "They're about to pass around the apple shine. Can I bring ye a sip?"

"I'd take one," said Cal. "Been seven years or more and I've been dreamin' about it ever since."

"Make that two, please," said Charlie.

Abigail disappeared into the swelling crowd.

"Wasn't that odd?" said Cal.

Charlie shrugged.

"It's all a little odd if you ask me."

"Maybe she saw you takin' pictures and thought I was famous."

"She knew who you were, though. Maybe she's had too much to drink."

"Didn't seem drunk to me. Sure liked my dress an awful lot."

"Seeing what everyone else is wearing, you must look like the Queen of Sheba to her."

Cal covered up.

"Is it too much?"

"No, not at all," said Charlie. "I put my foot in my mouth. You look great."

"I've got a foot for you," she said, and kicked him.

Abigail returned shortly with a pair of jelly jars, a caramel-colored liquid inside. She presented them with an air of royalty.

"The shine is strong this year," she said. "But they been keepin' it cool in the creek all day long. Goes down gentler that way. A hot hooch'll hit your stomach and shoot right back out again."

Charlie swallowed a small mouthful and for a moment he didn't know which direction it was headed. "You weren't kidding," he said. "Like a kick in the tail."

"Don't mind him," said Cal. "He's a city boy. Maybe we can find him a glass of warm goat milk." She took a sip and fluttered her eyelids. "Lord, that's even better than I remembered."

They passed around golden squares of cornbread and steaming wicker bowls brimming with potato cakes and smoked pork ribs. The moonshine flowed and the voices in the crowd grew louder. A reed flute, a fiddler, and a large drum made an unlikely trio as the villagers ate and danced and a general inebriation settled over the crowd. The sun had fallen just below the treetops when the church bell tolled again. The children sat on the grass and the rest filed into the rows of bleachers. When the bell tones quieted, a woman's voice came drifting from the orchard. A beautiful song, hushed by the trees. An elderly woman with long silver hair appeared among the old grey branches. Around her neck hung a braided necklace weighted with a bird skull. She sang with her arms reaching, beaded leather shoes gliding over the grass.

"Who is that?" whispered Charlie. He was watching the woman through the eyepiece of the 8 mm camera with the tiny hand-cranked motor thrumming. When Cal didn't answer, he turned and saw that her eyes were full of tears. There were others crying, too. They listened and watched with tinseled eyes.

"It's Gertrudis," she said. "That old woman I told you about. Hasn't aged a day. Ain't she just an angel? Didn't know she could sing like that."

The woman sang of ships and sea fog. She sang of lost kinship and the moon's silver eyes. Of roots winding through dark highland clay and fruit that grows red and round and sweet. She lulled the audience with her voice as if by spellcraft. When she ended her song, someone handed her a torch and lit it. She held the flame aloft as it sputtered and smoked and then she wedged it into kindling's latticework. As the fire grew, the children rose and gathered around her.

"This is the part I remember," said Cal. She dried her eyes on Charlie's shoulder and took another sip from the jelly jar. "I used to do this as a little girl."

"Do what?"

"Just get your camera ready."

Charlie put the camera to his eye.

Gertrudis lifted her hands into the air as the children giggled and nudged each other playfully. She waited till she had their complete attention and then she clapped her hands together three times. The children began to scream and contort. Wild, piercing screams. They growled at the villagers and stalked them with gnashing teeth. Some fell to their sides and writhed in the grass like snakes. Others reared up and pounced on invisible objects. They tore clods of dirt out of the grass and threw them into the air with the earth falling all around them.

Charlie's eyes drifted toward Cal as the camera whirred.

"This is normal?" he said.

"Just watch."

When the hysteria reached its peak, Gertrudis clapped again.

One by one, the children went crawling and hopping into the orchard. Their wild cries subsided, and for a moment, an eerie silence settled over the village. The only sound was the crackle of the great fire. The crowd seemed to be waiting for something to happen. You could see people shifting in their seats and cupping their ears. Then, from somewhere deep in the orchard, the children sang the Song of the Red Squire. They repeated the rhymes three times and then all was quiet again. When they reappeared, each was smiling and drinking from a clay mug. Gertrudis patted them on the head and the audience returned to a relaxed and casual state.

"It's the sweet cider I told you about," said Cal.

Charlie set the camera in his lap.

"I've never seen anything like that."

"Reckon you won't ever again."

The sun had fallen deep below the treetops and a chill settled over the village. Many were drunk, circling the fire in a wild dance to the fiddler's tune. Staccato handclaps sent more of them rising up from their seats and around the fire, faces warped in the yellow flames.

"Come dance with me, Charlie," said Cal. She was swaying and twirling the hem of her dress with a big pretty smile.

"You go ahead, I'll watch."

"Come on, Charlie."

"Maybe in a bit."

"Well, all right. Don't go gettin' jealous if you see me dancin' with somebody."

"Go on, have fun," he said. He felt a slight numbness on his lips from the moonshine, warmth flushing his neck and cheeks. He knew she felt it too. "I'll move closer so I can watch you dance."

"What kind of fake husband are you, anyhow?" She'd taken a playful tone. "Won't even dance with your fake wife."

"If you saw me dance, you'd ask for a fake divorce."

"Suit yourself." She stuck out her tongue and went spinning off toward the bonfire, joining the circle of dancers while the bright orange dome of the harvest moon leered over the treetops. He filmed her while she danced. He thought she looked so beautiful with her wild hair twirling, eyes catching the firelight just so.

The Scrivener appeared with an empty burlap sack, the girl Margaret trailing a few steps behind. There was an official quality in the way they approached.

"You and your wife enjoyin' yourselves, Squire?" said the Scrivener.

Charlie began to stand, but the Scrivener waved him back down.

"We are," he said. "I shot a few rolls of film, and I'll do some measurements before we leave in the morning."

"That is acceptable." The Scrivener eyed the 8 mm in Charlie's hand. "I thought maybe you'd forgotten your poke, so I brought ye one. The Sun has set and the Moon is risin' up."

Charlie took the burlap sack and looked it over. "If it's all the same, I'll just put it back into my camera duffel."

"Please do. Then put the duffel into this'n here, per our agreement."

Charlie nodded and began to settle his equipment.

"Is the festival over?"

The Scrivener chuckled softly.

"It ain't over till the food and hooch runs out. Besides, we ain't even seen that pesky ol' Hellekyn. Looks like theys settin' up for it now." There was a man erecting a row of torches that ran from the orchard to the fire pit.

"Hellekyn?"

"One of our oldest traditions, but not for the children to see. They'll all be put to bed soon. That includes you, Margaret."

Margaret stood watching the torch lighter with a glassy stare.

"Wouldn't want to see that old Hellekyn anyhow," she said. "Goin' to bed is just fine with me." When she said it, a loud cackle erupted from the orchard and the music stopped. The dancers slowed and turned toward the sound, chests rising and falling. The children in the crowd began to stir, and some of the older villagers were ushering them off to their shacks. "I'm goin' home now," said Maragret.

Again, the cackle. Then, a loud snap like the crack of a whip.

As the children went running to their homes, the adults drifted back to the benches and took their seats. The cackling alternated with howls and grunting, growing louder and louder. Cal returned, hair clinging to her forehead with sweat. She found her jelly jar under the seat and slammed a mouthful down her throat.

"You remember any of this?" said Charlie.

She shook her head and glanced over the orchard, searching for the source of the cackling.

"My grandad said there was a clown in the orchard that came out after the festival. But it weren't anything for a child to see. He told us about it like it was some kind of ghost story."

A man and woman filtered through the crowd, refilling everyone's jelly jars. After they made their rounds, the man stood atop one of the benches and raised his drink.

"To the Hellekyn," said the man, to which everyone booed and hissed. "The drunker we are, the better we'll fare."

The crowd drank.

Charlie raised his glass to Cal.

"I don't know what's going on, but I sure wish I could film it."

"Just do what everyone else is doin'. Don't call attention to yourself."

They both drank.

A wild fiddle tune erupted, anchored by the beat of a loud and bassy drum. A woman in the front row vomited and was quickly ushered out into the darkness. Another man added two armfuls of logs to the fire. Sparks shot up spinning and winking out against the stars. The song played, the drumming grew louder. A loud cry like a coyote yip came three times and the music suddenly dropped out. A long-legged figure stepped from the orchard, wearing a hornet's nest mask—a bald and featureless dome of chewed mud. Tiny eyelets sat dark and round, and there was a mouthhole just large enough to accommodate a long, wet tongue. It came loping slowly, weaving around the row of torches with its arms reaching and clawing at the crowd. The Hellekyn's bare chest was painted with black and white diamonds and the hands were red as bird feathers. It thrust its hips at the fire, and from the waist a trio of small gourds jangled.

The man who offered the toast rose slowly with his palms showing, as one might approach a horse about to spook.

"What is your name?" asked the man.

The Hellekyn darted its tongue as he drew near, like a snake tasting the air. The man leaned in, and the Hellykyn scrambled up close and whispered into the man's ear. The man nodded in understanding.

"Ladies and gentlemen," said the man, as the drumming grew louder. "I present to you, Mr. Goat Ass!"

The Hellekyn growled and tore off one of the gourds from its leather belt and shook it in the air. It went from person to person, pressing its face close and taking long, dramatic whiffs as if drawing out their very souls. It sniffed and snorted. Then it threw its thumblike head back, cackled into the sky, and moved on.

"You been drinkin' the 'shine, haven't you?" whispered Cal.

"Maybe not as much as I should have been. Didn't know there'd be a test."

"Well, drink up."

It approached Cal with a hulking, spider-like movement. The eyes stared down and the tongue came out. It lifted her chin and leaned in. An almost romantic gesture. When it pulled away, the thing grunted and shook its head.

The crowd groaned.

"What do I do now?" said Cal.

The Hellekyn pinched a tiny stopper from the gourd and a ruddy liquid welled from the hole. He lifted it to her mouth.

"Open," was the cry from the crowd. "Open up!"

Cal parted her lips and the liquid dribbled into her mouth.

It turned to Charlie and repeated the ritual with the same outcome.

"Open," they called again.

Charlie resisted.

The crowd rose and booed, shaking their fists and stomping.

"Just drink it," said Cal.

"What is it?"

"Tastes like some kind of tea," said Cal, "but with booze." She was so drunk that she could barely get the words out.

Charlie opened his mouth and took the liquid. The Hellekyn chortled triumphantly and scuttled to the next row. When it had reached the last person, it ran a crazed lap around the fire and sprinted into the orchard.

"What did you think?" asked Cal.

"Like chamomile," said Charlie. The word came out mealy and strange. "With a bite, though." He was watching the place in the trees where the Hellekyn had gone, shaking his head. "I didn't think this could get any stranger. They're never going to believe this back home."

Then he heard the goats.

The Hellekyn reappeared, commanding a half-dozen goats by the clicks of its teeth. They walked upright on their hind legs in a strange, man-like waddle, heads bobbing and shimmying like horses, their hooves clomping in the grass. Their forelegs dangled uselessly as they trundled along like followers of some long-lost druidic order. The Hellekyn led them twice around the great fire as the crowd made goat sounds of their own, and then they returned single file to the orchard amid a chorus of parting bleats.

Someone shouted:

"So long, Goat Ass!" and everyone erupted with laughter.

Soon after, two men appeared with pinewood barrels and filled the great fire pit with water. Steam twisted in the woodsmoke. After seven or eight bucket loads, water spilled from the rim of the pit and the fire subtracted to a greenish-blue flame and faded completely. Full of cornbread and liquor, the villagers sprawled in the grass and watched the moon succumb to a slow, inky shadow that spread like oil on white linen. The faintest of stars now shined bright as diamond dust.

Come now, Squire. Watch the moon, now reddened in earth's clockwork swing. Watch eons of soot churn at the galactic core. Count the sisters of the Pleiades, adrift in a milkcloud above the hunter's bow. Find the face you seek in the reeling of zodiacs and the venial flow of nebulae. Sit drunk and ghostlike in that monochrome gloom where shadows lay atop shadows. Come now, Squire. Soon the virgin moon will find you in her newly woken eye. Raise the sword and swing it true. How deep the roots twist beneath that highland clay. How deep, how deep? Can you hear the lute's jangle and strum? The chord's blue reverb? Somewhere the sound of water chimes like a coin flicked into a deep cavern. Fossil bones pommeled in the dank earthen walls. From the cavemouth comes a long carbonate sigh. Hear its voice. Come now, Squire. The raven spreads her wings, and the jack has fled the briar. The Chessman will soon take a Queen—and she will bear the Maiden fruit.

They staggered to the shack on numb legs, falling twice to the ground before reaching the door. He helped her undress and tucked the sheets and blankets around her as she lay mumbling. She rolled toward the wall with the blanket pulled to her chin and began to snore. Charlie fumbled with the gas lamp on the table, but was too drunk to light it. He went outside and sat against the shack and smoked, watching the night sky.

Moonlight had returned and filled the village with a strange metallic pallor. Mist sifted through the trees, growing thicker as he sat and watched. He finished his cigarette and lit another, concentrating very hard on the apple trees to stop his head from spinning. The way the vapors played with the starlight captivated him.

He opened the shack door and peered inside. Cal lay peacefully in the bed. He found his duffel and removed the 35 mm camera, checked the frame counter dial. Only four shots taken on the roll. He hung the camera strap around his neck, knocking the cigarette onto the floor in a shower of red sparks. He picked it up, placed it between his lips and went out into the night. No wind at all, not even the slightest breeze. He started down through the orchard and continued until he found the stone pedestal. He looked over the range-finder and could barely read the numbers on the face of it. With his old war Zippo lit, he found the shutter speed lever, set it for a time exposure, and rested the camera on the pedestal. The lens pointed down the rows of apple trees with the mist flowing through the branches. He clicked the shutter open and counted to ten and released it. Then again at twenty seconds, and a third time at thirty.

He saw a faint yellow glow at the far end of the orchard. Perhaps a lantern. He edged toward it. The light dimmed and brightened again as if something passed in between. He heard the sound of shovels ticking in the soil. Charlie crouched at the edge of the orchard, just beyond the rim of the lamplight, watching for movement. He crept closer still. Faces emerged from the dark, some of them wearing elaborate costumes. Masks that sat tall and square on the shoulders, as if built upon the bones of apple crates. Strap leather hung from the top and bottom to simulate hair and the faces were fashioned with white linen. Long bent noses, mouthless chins. They stood in a half-circle around an excavated hole with dead hares hanging from the branches. Beside the hole, a skeleton lay wrapped in a black and white blanket.

He raised the camera and clicked a photograph, advanced the roll.

A maskless woman dragged the bones to the edge of the hole and the group spoke together in unison. Hushed voices. Hands outstretched. As they murmured together, the maskless ones inched the skeleton closer to the hole until it tipped over the rim and fell away. Shovelers came and filled the grave, the spades of their shovels casting shadows all around them. A heavy mist blew in and out of the scene. When the dirt had risen, someone brought a sapling and set it atop the grave while the shovelers filled and packed more dirt around it.

Charlie took another photograph.

The chanting now had an ominous quality about it, and all the masked ones had retreated into the shadows except one. The remaining figure stood over the sapling, whispering. It tilted its cube mask to the moon with the leather straps falling around its shoulders, palms upturned. From behind, many hands slipped over the legs and torso. Men's and women's hands alike. They fluttered from the feet to his chest and back down again. They unfastened the clasps at the waist and the trousers inched slowly down. A long dark phallus hung in the bare glow of the lantern. The hands fluttered over his thighs and stomach. They took him up and worked back and forth. The whispers grew, the movement quickened.

Charlie snapped another photo.

Faster now.

The masked figure was breathing loudly, straddling the sapling.

Knees buckling.

Rising up on his toes.

A gasp and a long exhale.

As the figure came over the sapling, Charlie inched forward to take another photo and his numb, half-drunk legs sent him sideways against the apple tree. A branch snapped, and when he righted himself, he looked up to see the ceremony faces watching him in the dark.

Charlie turned and ran.

He cut through the center of the orchard with the sounds of footsteps all around him. They were shouting, commanding him to stop. He weaved through the trees as he ran, the weight of the night's booze still heavy in his legs. He reached the back of the orchard where the dead black trees stood and veered left toward the shack.

He stopped.

A masked figure stood before him, blocking his path.

Long nose hooking downward.

Another to his left.

"Give me the camera, Charlie," said the closest figure.

The voice sounded familiar. He'd heard it recently.

Charlie dangled the camera by the strap and slowly handed it over.

"Beech? Is that you?"

The figure took the camera and bobbed it between them as if guessing its weight. A right hook sent Charlie peddling back and falling to the dirt. A kick to the gut, then another. He tried to get up, but the beating wouldn't quit. Charlie was trying to apologize when the camera hooked up into the air and came down hard across his face. He felt bones crack, tasted blood as it poured into his mouth. The camera came up a second time and caught him square in the jaw. On the third swing, another figure stopped it from coming down.

"That's enough," said a voice.

It was the last thing he heard before his eyes slammed shut.

He woke alone, slumped over the stone pedestal with blood trailing from his mouth into the carved inscriptions. The only sounds were the slight ringing in his ears and a chorus of crickets from somewhere beyond the orchard. He pushed himself up and rubbed his jaw. His cheek felt fractured. Nose broken. He could hardly open his mouth without lightning forks of pain.

He steadied himself on a tree branch, one eye swollen to a wink.

The shirt he wore was not his own. In place of the crisp white button-up, he now wore a wool tunic like the other inhabitants of Wyldton. Only this one was as red as the apples in the orchard.

He found his way to the wooden shack and pulled open the door.

"Cal," he said, searching for her in the dark. "Cal, we have to go."

He found the Zippo lighter in his pocket and spun the sparkwheel.

She hung over the side of the bed with a pool of cornbread vomit on the floor. Her bag was open and her clothes had been strewn all over the shack.

"Cal," he said, louder this time. His jaw ached when he spoke. The pain made his eyes water. "We have to leave now."

He jostled her and she stirred, groaning. "Charlie?"

"Yeah, it's me." He glanced out the window as if he could sense them watching. He touched his jaw tenderly. "I made a mistake and we need to leave. They fucked me up pretty bad."

She curled in the bed and wept. There was vomit in her hair and she couldn't keep her eyes open.

"Charlie, why'd you bring me here?"

"You're not making sense. Come on, let's go."

She choked and vomited in the bed.

He tore off the red tunic and found a shirt and sweater in the overnight bag and put them on. He unzipped the camera duffel and looked inside. The spent rolls of film were still inside the bag along with the Revere 88. He collected everything and threw the carry straps over his shoulder.

He tried to rouse Cal again, but she only tossed and moaned.

The smell was unbearable.

"I'm going to get the truck and bring it straight up the trail," said Charlie. "I won't leave you. I brought you here and I'll bring you back. I promise."

He watched her in the Zippo's flickering light.

She hadn't heard a word of it.

Charlie fled down the row of shacks toward the exit trail. The sky was clear and full of moonlight. He saw movement in his periphery, but he pretended it wasn't there. Straight across the village to the trail as fast as he could walk. He came to the swirling flagstones with their chalky glyphs and passed through the fir grove where mist hung in the branches like spiderwebs. He ignored the sounds he heard out there beyond the treeline. The scuffs in the dead needles, the popping of twigs. The murmurs and sharp whispers. He knew they were watching him. When he entered the clearing, he went straight to the pickup, threw open the door, and cranked the ignition.

The flywheel spun, but the engine wouldn't turn over.

He cussed and tried again.

He smelled gasoline. Not the faint smell of an engine flooding, but the sharp scent of fresh gas right under his nose. He planted his foot down and it made a tiny splash. Charlie jumped out of the truck and looked closely at the pedals. Everything was wet and reeked of gasoline. He popped the hood and peered into the engine compartment.

Sitting atop the carburetor was another hideous apple doll.

He took the doll and held it to the sky.

The bells on the jumper rang.

"Is this some kind of game?" he called to the trees.

The murmurs grew. Figures passing behind the tree trunks.

Charlie returned to the cab of the truck and scrubbed the doll head against the floorboards. He passed the Zippo beneath it and set it alight, holding it torchlike into the air. The light of the flaming doll brightened the trees. Some of the villagers didn't bother to hide. He watched them and they watched him back. Blank mannequin faces staring in the torchlight. He reached into the truck and honked his horn while the doll's head hissed and sputtered. Sweet smell of burning fruit.

"The festival's over," he shouted. "You're all a bunch of crazy sonsabitches!"

He tossed the doll out into the night and began to rummage through the other vehicles, looking for car keys. He flipped visors and opened gloveboxes, digging through every compartment he could find. When he couldn't get any of the cars started, he went back up the trail, talking to the trees all the while.

"Try to stop me," he was saying. "I'm going to get Cal and get the hell out here. Hear me? Try to stop us, you crazy fuckers!"

They jeered and taunted from the shadows as he hurried through the village to the wooden shack. He threw open the door and clapped his hands.

"Come on, Cal," he said. "I'll carry you if I have to but we're getting out of here now." He lit the oil lamp on the table and waved the lighter around in the dark while it sputtered and glowed.

The shack was empty.

The sheets had been stripped and there was no trace of Cal.

He turned to the door, but it slammed shut before he could grab it.

The handle wouldn't budge.

Charlie screamed and pounded with the heel of his hand.

"Let me out, you goddamn lunatics," he cried.

He felt his nerves twist, every pore weeping with sweat. He kicked at the door and caromed from wall to wall like some conserved maniac. One of Oswyn's wooden figurines toppled from the shelf and he scooped it up and chucked it at the window. The glass blew out and he began working the shards out of the sill. He managed to remove a long, blade-like piece when a form appeared in the window. He recoiled, and the glass slipped from his hands and shattered on the floor. The Hellekyn stood peering through the empty space with its hornet's nest mask and slick red tongue wagging from the hole. That eerie bald face like the teat of a nannygoat. It growled and cried and shook its gourds. Goats bleated from every direction. Charlie heard them tromping in circles around the shack, scraping their horns on the siding. They marched behind the Hellekyn with their barred pupils and dark lashes wetly shining.

Charlie sat on the bare mattress with his head in his hands. The carnival of sounds and emotions overtook him. A sick feeling churned in his guts. Something hot and jagged stirred there. He felt it rise and burn at the pit of his throat. He doubled over and retched but nothing came. The oil lamp cast a strange scene over the walls. Figures of light dancing and tumbling. They came and went with the flicker of the lamp, a court of demented fools and loping animals. He suddenly felt he was in a very large room and he was just a doll on a toy bed, watching a broken projector shove images onto the walls. Faces everywhere. He saw them in the burls and knots of wood in the floorboards. He saw them in the woolen tweed fibers of the mattress. He saw them in the folds of his palm and in the sparse whorls of hair on the backs of his knuckles.

He held up a hand as if blocking the high noon sun.

"End this madness," he cried.

"This madness has no end," replied a chorus of voices.

Smaller still. Charlie found himself in the microscopic topography of the pinewood floor, ridged and valleyed like the grooves of a vinyl record. A mouse femur lay tangled in a wad of dust with mites scuttling in the loomwork, their great nightmarish chelicerae scissoring as they foraged. A sliver of glass settled close by, webbed and striated. Or maybe a grain of salt. It held pockets of pure white light within a crystalline lattice. A finger of blood came runnelling down the pinewood grooves and he looked up where a pile of bodies lay stacked in the corner of the room beneath a bayonet's labor. He heard metal strike bone, saw the blood chum fouling the tapered steel blade as the bayonet rose and fell.

"Stop, please," he cried.

This time there was no reply.

The nausea hit again. Hot liquid rising. He coughed and choked until it finally came up in a mess on the floor. In the pool of digestive fluid he saw a half-dozen codling moth larvae squirming and rearing up. The sight of it made him retch again. More larvae came. They wormed and writhed in the shiny grease and trailed off into the dark gaps between the flooring and disappeared.

He felt his conscious mind slipping toward someplace darker and quieter. He heard the drumming of his heart over a thin white sound like radio static. He welcomed it. Familiar voices faded in and out. He saw fragments of his life trembling at the edges of some undefined space. An outline of his mother's profile came and went. His sister's face. A brother. He saw a young girl with messy blond hair and a bloody cotton dress floating above the fir trees, waving her arms. *"Herkommen,"* she whispered. *"Herkommen, Charlie."*

The images sank into a heavy black void.

Someplace far beyond sleep but not too distant yet.

———

He woke to a faint greyness in the broken window, a raven prattling nearby. He could still hear his heart drumming in his chest, or maybe it was a drumbeat from some other place entirely. He listened for it. It came and went. The oil in the lamp had long sputtered out. He sat in the cold semi-dark and looked himself over. His face was painfully swollen, and he was wearing the red tunic again. All the other items had disappeared from the room. His camera bag, spare clothes. Cal's things were gone, too. He rose and shuffled to the door and peered out. Aster petals lay in the dirt among the goat turds and broken glass. He looked around for movement, but no one was about.

"Cal," he called. His voice sounded alien to himself, and the motion hurt his jaw. "Cal, where are you?"

He went down the row of shacks and peered into the windows. The village felt abandoned. He passed the benches where the festival had taken place. Pork ribs lay scattered in the grass. Shards of broken jelly jars. The morning still held much of the night air. He thought for a moment he heard the drumming again and he cocked his ear but couldn't place it from any direction.

He toed at the door of the Scrivener's shack. It opened with a lilting groan as if an awkward question had been asked. He scanned the room once for the Scrivener, and a second time for Margaret. He found neither. He lifted an antique flintlock rifle from the wall and worked the hammer up and down against the pan. There was a Latin inscription on the riflestock that he could not make out. It looked like something a conquistador would use to defend a Spanish fort. He returned the rifle and lifted a sword from a forked bracket on the wall. He held it with one hand on the grip and the other on the scabbard and he unsheathed the blade with a long whispering sound. It wasn't as heavy as it looked. A blue-looking blade, long and thin. He brought it into the morning light and swung it low and steady through the air.

The drumming quickened. Louder now. He thought it was coming from the far end of the apple orchard. He started across the village with the hilt at his waist and the tip of the sword raised like a knight in some forgotten fairy tale. He stopped to listen. The sound grew and receded, but it never completely faded. He continued past the old dead trees until he came to a sheer wall of limestone. He could see the hemlock tree far above him where Oswyn's bones had lain. He followed the cliff face as it angled down along a rocky trail that switchbacked below the village. He could almost hear the drumskin rattling with each beat. The chords of a stringed instrument ringing. He was close now. The trail made a hairpin around the cliff face and ended beneath the dark yawning mouth of a cave. He went on. A thin grey smoke sputtered from the cave entrance. Light played against the walls. He could see people standing inside, still as wax figures.

Charlie crept into the dark of the cave with the sword tip leading. The villagers stood against the cavewalls, some in normal dress and some with the ornate apple crate masks from the night before. Some held torches. The air felt slick and the forms surrounding him had an iridescent sheen as if he was entering some other time and place. He saw the Scrivener crouched at a little wooden desk with a fuming black candle, holding a quill pen.

"Where is she?" said Charlie. "I'm not leaving without her."

The cave was now silent, save for the sound of water gurgling through fissures of rock.

"Answer me, goddamn you."

"You're too late, Squire," said the Scrivener. Others said it too. It became an echo that repeated throughout the cavern. The Scrivener checked a silver pocket-watch and noted the time in a ledger. "Three minutes past seven."

"Where is she?"

The Scrivener gazed into the great basilica where long roots dangled as thick as horse tongues. Something stirred there. Charlie swiped a torch from a villager and elbowed through the roots toward the center of the cave. Beneath him lay a stone grid with piles of bones stacked inside the squares as if he walked atop some centuries-old board game frozen in time. A drip fell on the back of his hand. Another on his scalp. He gazed into the center of the root mass. A woman hung face down in the brambles with her arms outstretched like a magician's trick. Blond hair falling downward. The roots were slick here, dark and wet.

Charlie called to her. She responded with the faintest of groans.

Blood trickled down her arms and gathered at her fingertips.

He batted his way through until he stood directly beneath her. She lay ten feet up, blue dress now stained black. There were leaves deckled between her teeth like book pages. One of the roots coiled around a dark, glistening organ and another was probing a wound in her abdomen. Smaller tendrils ran along the back of her scalp and into her ears like a pair of cradling hands.

Charlie laid the tip off the blade over the Scrivener's toadlike eye.

"What the hell did you do to her?"

The Scrivener gazed calmly over the blade tip.

"You've got to feed the Devil, Squire."

"Enough bullshit. Bring her down."

"It's too late. You could have saved her, but it's too late. It has already taken what it wanted."

"Goddamnit, bring her down."

"You're the one with the sword, Squire. But I'd use restraint if I were ye."

Charlie spun on his heels and hacked at a long tassel of roots. The cut pieces coiled on the ground and a blackish substance began to leak and squirt from the severed ends. Some of it splashed over Charlie's arms and it felt like boiling hot grease. A sharp clicking sound erupted and the whole root mass quavered. Cal dropped a few inches in the tangle, her limbs slack and lifeless. He struck again, this time cutting off larger pieces, maybe seven feet of it at a time. He shoved the torch at the curtain of roots to the sounds of hissing and popping.

Dirt rained down from the dark of the cavern.

The cavewalls rumbled.

"You shouldn't have done that," said the Scrivener. "It was too late to save her anyhow. Now you'll have to fight it."

"Fight what?"

The villagers joined together in groups for protection. Some fled into the daylight.

"The Chessman," said the Scrivener, flicking the quill pen. "And you cannot win."

A tangled mass moved through the roots like a spider in a web. A woody, knotted thing. When it touched the ground, it cambered formlessly along the cavern as if undecided on what shape it should take. It looked like a giant woodrat's nest that had come alive, or perhaps a ball of writhing snakes. From its center, a leathery pod like a woman's handbag unwound and buoyed in the air. A face took shape there—two black pupils and an arrow-like nose. A beard of moss grew beneath a tightly drawn rictus. The pod fattened and the face grew large. Something like a Byzantine portrait etched into rawhide.

Cal was now dangling haphazardly in her blood-soaked dress.

A voice came, or something approximating voice. A backwards sucking sound that clacked and groaned from some long-silent organ. Then came a shuddering whisper like tree leaves and the reek of compost filled the air.

"Who is't challenges me?"

Charlie worked his jaw, but no words came.

The slithering knot loomed above him, clicking and hissing.

"I challenge you," said Charlie. "Bring her down, now."

"Which king doth thou s'rve, Squire?" it said.

Charlie spat. "I serve no king."

"Which gods, then?"

"I give the same answer."

"Well, then. An apostate bef're all gods art thou?"

A root shot from its core and coiled tightly around Charlie's throat. Another searched beneath his tunic at a spot beneath his ribs.

"Then I shall sup thy heathen liv'r beside the maiden fruit. A bite f'r a bite. A sour m'rsel to balance the sweet. I shalt maketh a rook of thy bones and place thee atop the board."

Charlie lifted off the ground, toes barely touching the floor. The speed of its tendrils had caught him by surprise. His esophagus sealed shut. He felt the blood swelling in his eyes and cheeks. He grabbed the slick root with one hand and sawed with the blade. His vision had nearly tunneled to black when the cut followed through. He broke free, dropped to his feet, and thrust the sword into the pod face. A gush of red-black liquid poured from the wound and the thing reeled back shrieking with its roots whipping the air. Another pod bloomed from the mass and a different, angrier face began to take shape there.

"Look what you've done," said the Scrivener. "Now it will kill us all."

The walls shook and more debris rained down. Charlie backed slowly into the daylight with black grease sliding down the blade. Villagers shouldered past him on all sides. The thing lumbered after him, folding through the cave mouth with its roots grasping at the sides of the cliff face like an octopus exiting its den. Charlie inched up the trail toward the village, watching it completely unfold into the daylight. It seemed to drag the darkness out of the cave along with it, carrying the shadows like a brood. Villagers careened off the trail into the rosebay hells, apple crate masks falling from their shoulders as they fled. The thing took a man by the leg and whipped him against the side of the cliff. He toppled dead on the trail with his head split and pulpy. It flung a woman into the air and she went screaming over the treetops.

Charlie hustled up the grade and the thing followed close behind. When he reached the great orchard, it caught him by the ankle and flipped him sideways into the dirt. The sword nearly fell from his hand. Where it touched his skin, a wound opened and blood poured out. He swung the sword two-handedly and again broke free. He scrambled to his feet and hobbled across the village and down the flagstone path. The thing tore branches from the fir trees as it went, the ropes of its manifold body slapping at the stones behind him. He reached the clearing and saw the Ford truck with the door slightly ajar and he ran to it, climbed inside, and shut it tight.

The key sat in the ignition where he'd left it.

The Chessman rolled atop the hood of the truck with unholy ease, wet clay and blood smearing onto the glass as it peered inside. The pod face blistered into vaguely humanoid features, eyes drawing down upon Charlie like a wax bishop from a pulpit. It battered the glass until a star pattern bloomed over the windshield.

Charlie kicked the clutch pedal and dropped the shifter to neutral.

The truck began to roll.

The Chessman struck again, and glass rained over the dash. It was trying to fit into the small hole it had made, prying a whitish thorn at the glass.

Charlie reached across the cab and rolled the passenger window down.

The truck rolled faster now, backwards along the rut road.

The thing sensed the opening and began to slide inside the cab, pulling itself onto the passenger door. He turned the ignition. The flywheel whined and the hot smell of gasoline flooded the cab. He could see it spraying from the fuel lines onto the floor where the villagers had committed their sabotage. It mixed with the blood from the gash in his leg.

Vines snaked along the dash. Beetle grubs dropped onto the seats, scurrying for places to hide. The cab darkened, and an oily sheen rippled over the remaining window glass. The Chessman's body was too large to fit through the window, but it was vicious and determined. The sheet metal groaned and glass crackled inside the door. It ripped and tore until the door puckered inward, and the thing slid its face beside Charlie's.

"Thy chariot is no sanctuary, Squire," it hissed.

The truck bounced and jolted over the road.

Engine heaving.

The stench of rot and petrol.

"Consider it your fucking tomb, demon," he said.

Charlie opened the driver door and stepped onto the running board. He flicked open the Zippo, spun the sparkwheel, and tossed it onto the floor. Bright orange flames rolled through the cab. He felt the heat on his face as he lunged onto the road and toppled into the field grass. The Chessman shrieked and flailed with rage. It was trying to force its way back out the window when the truck careened off the road and wrecked into a stand of fir trees. Black smoke welled from the truck's windows. He could see a flurry of movement there. Flaming vines reaching for the tree branches. The firs began to catch fire, too, and soon the heat and flames and the roiling smoke obscured everything. The trees drew inward, and a piercing shriek erupted. The sound rolled out across the hills and echoed off the crags and scree slopes up on the ridgeline. A dark cloud gathered briefly over the crash site, then flattened to a thin white mist.

Charlie pushed himself to his feet.

Some of the villagers were gathering in the cul-de-sac, watching the flames grow. One by one, they picked stones out of the grass and began to throw them at Charlie. They landed out of reach, making little grey puffs where they struck the earth. They screamed and ranted like a gang of asylum wards. He couldn't make out what they were saying. After they'd driven him farther down the road, they huddled together with their arms draped over each other's shoulders and began to pray.

To which god was anyone's guess.

—————

The rut road angled down the hill, winding onward along the creek through the fir trees and toward the old mountain highway. Blood seeped into his shoe, and it made a sucking sound as he limped onward. By the time he reached the main road, he was leaving dark footprints behind him. The air had grown bitter cold. He shuffled along with his arms folded and chin tucked to conserve warmth. He stopped every few miles and looked up and down the road, waiting for a passing car, but none came. As the elevation dropped and the morning wore on, the temperature kept falling. Snow flurries corkscrewed over the road. He stopped before a large sugar maple and stared into its barren matrix of branches where only yesterday leaves hung red and plentiful.

The sound of a car engine came drifting down the mountain road.

Charlie stuck out his thumb and waited.

A black Chevy truck let off the gas when it hit the straightaway, slowing to a stop along the shoulder. Charlie in his wool tunic opened the passenger door and climbed in. His teeth were chattering so hard he could barely say a word of thanks.

"Son, you look about half-froze," said the driver. He was an older man, clean-shaven. Big white brows over pale blue eyes. He kept glancing at Charlie as if each new detail alarmed him more than the last. "You're bleedin' all over the floor. You pick a fight with a bear?"

"J-just take me to the t-train station," Charlie managed.

"Train station? Reckon you need more than a train ride. A hospital might be a better choice."

"P-please, sir. I don't want to miss my train."

The old man pulled onto the highway, shaking his head.

"I got in the habit of pickin' up soldiers after the war, but I should have stuck with uniformed men."

"I f-fought in the war," said Charlie. He was rubbing his hands against the heater vent under the dash. "Army infantry. Th-thanks for the ride."

"No offense, son. But it looks like you fought in all the wars at once. You get lost huntin' out here?"

Charlie sidled his eyes at the old man, hoping some reasonable explanation would manifest on his tongue.

"Lost, y-yeah."

A few minutes passed, and the old man straightened in his seat as if something important had occurred to him.

"Say, you the fella that disappeared up here a few months back? You and that woman from West Jefferson?"

Charlie shook his head.

"No. Drove up yesterday. Truck broke down is all. Got lost trying to find the highway."

When they passed the town of Fig, Charlie noticed a large, decorated Christmas tree standing in front of the old church where Cal had given her donation. A wreath hung in the doorway. He couldn't stop shaking. Whether it was from the cold or just his rattling nerves, he couldn't tell.

"I'm going to pull into this here liquor store," said the man.

"I really don't want to miss my train."

"I'll be right quick."

"Can you keep the heater running?"

The man looked as if a big favor had been asked.

"Long as you promise not to go joyridin'."

"Do I look like I want to go joyriding?"

"Son, if I told you what you looked like, it'd be a hell of a long mornin'."

A minute later, he came out with a younger blond man who was holding something in his hand. The man came around to the passenger side door and motioned for Charlie to roll the window down. He held a photograph with writing over the bottom of the image. When the window came down, he studied the photograph and flicked his eyes back and forth.

"You Charles Danwitter?" said the blond man.

Charlie was trying to get a glimpse of the photograph.

"What is that?"

He showed him. It was a USDA identification photo with a five-hundred-dollar reward notice for information leading to his whereabouts.

"I don't understand," said Charlie.

"Looks like you've had a rough go of it," said the blond man. "Why don't you wait with Carl here. I'm goin' to call for help."

"My train leaves this afternoon," said Charlie. "I just want to go home."

"Your train? Reckon you're a tad confused."

"It leaves at noon. I can't miss it."

The blond man chuckled and exchanged glances with Carl.

"You have your train ticket on you?"

Charlie dug in his back pocket and opened his wallet. From the billfold, he removed his return ticket and showed the man. "See. Right here. It says twelve noon departure."

"Buddy, you done missed that train."

"What time is it?"

"Well, it ain't so much about the time. It's the day. Your train left over two months ago. Can't you see that Christmas tree? It's the middle of December."

Charlie abruptly opened the door and retched, but his stomach was empty.

The blond man hopped back. He nodded to Carl and then he disappeared into the liquor store. Carl reached in and killed the ignition and slipped the keys into his front pocket.

"It's gonna be all right, son. We're gettin' help now."

"I don't want help, I just want to go home."

"Got any idea where the girl is, Charles?"

He held his head in his hands and began to cry.

"They killed her."

"Who killed her?"

"They did."

———

Charlie woke just after sunrise to find Sheriff Danaver in full uniform sitting on a chair in the corner of the hospital room. He was watching Charlie thoughtfully with his lips pursed and one foot resting on his knee. He straightened and laced his fingers on his lap.

"Good mornin', Charlie," he said.

Charlie sat up in bed, IV tubes draping from a bag of saline.

"Morning," said Charlie.

"Spoke with the doc a few minutes ago."

"What'd he say?"

"With the right diet and exercise I could live to be ninety."

"Is that a joke?"

"Only if you think it's funny."

Charlie looked around the room. Vital monitors loomed over him. A bright window with billowing white curtains. A crucifix hung on each of the four walls and there was a statuette of Saint Mary on a table in the corner.

"Have you driven up to Wyldton yet?"

Danaver sat back with that ponderous look.

"It's the first place we looked. Beech Buchanan brought us up there when you both disappeared."

"Did you find Cal? Did you see what they did to her?"

Danaver shook his head.

"All we found was that burned out Ford truck rental of yours. Empty, of course."

"And the villagers?"

"Weren't nobody around. Beech reckons it's a seasonal camp for moonshiners now. Abandoned in the winter. Even though the law changed we still get plenty of moonshine camps up that way. There's a black market for everythin', I suppose."

"That's not true. He's lying. He was there."

"You sayin' Beech was with you?"

"I heard his voice. I know he's lying."

Danaver picked his cuticles.

"You probably haven't heard, but the Old Gambit burned down while you were missin'. Some say it was on purpose, but that's not how the fire inspector saw it."

"Did Beech get a payout?"

"Reckon he did. Left town this week."

"Well, there you go. He's lying about that, too."

"Wouldn't put it past him. Lord knows we've had plenty of misunderstandings between us. But I can usually smell a lie. It's part of the job."

"Listen to me, Sheriff. Must have been thirty or forty people up there. Maybe more if you count the children. All of them crazy as shit. It killed her, Sheriff. Damn near killed me, too."

"It? Last time we spoke, you had me confused about your choice of pronouns."

Charlie scrubbed his face with his palms.

"You won't believe me."

"Son, I seen my share of wicked shit in this county. There's an abandoned oil well up near Green Valley. Moonshiners used to dump bodies down the shaft. That was the rumor anyhow. I sent a contractor down there a few years back and he brought up three skulls. Human ones. I'll tell you somethin' not a lot of other people know about. One of them skulls had symbols carved into the back of it. Like those scrimshaw whale bones you see in the tourist shops down on the coast. Weren't no hack-job neither—they really put in the effort to do it right. I sent it off to the University down in Raleigh and they couldn't make heads nor tails of it. Real wicked shit, Charlie. So let's give it a shot. Give me all the fucked-up details."

Charlie fixed on the bright window for a long while.

"There was something down in the cave."

"What cave?"

"Below the town."

"Go on."

"Something evil. The villagers, they—" Charlie couldn't finish.

"Don't stop now, you're almost there."

"Well. It was like they fed her to this thing. It wanted her liver."

"Her liver?"

"That's right. I saw it take her liver."

"This thing. You talkin' like an animal, or—"

Charlie shook his head.

"Something else."

"Somethin' evil."

"That's right."

"Like a demonic spirit?"

"Yes. It lived in the roots. They fed her to it in some kind of ritual."

"Did you see these people? Were they moonshiners?"

"Not exactly. They just lived there. The Scrivener was one of them."

"The Scrivener?"

"It's an old term, I think. A Scrivener is someone who reads and writes and keeps track of information."

"I could use one of those around the office."

Charlie glared.

"I knew you wouldn't believe me."

Danaver rose and went slowly to Charlie's bedside. He reached into his pocket and pulled out a small glass vial full of pills.

"I spoke to old man Halbert down at the drugstore. Said you ordered this vial of Nembutal but never came back for it. Were you hopin' to get it refilled before you headed up the mountain?"

"I know where this is going. I'm not crazy, Sheriff."

"Didn't say you was crazy. I just need to know if you left with the girl and didn't have any of your medication on you."

"Yes."

"Yes what?"

"I didn't have the medication with me."

"I see. Have any episodes while you were up there? Your doctor called me too, you know. Dr. Young, ain't it? Smart as a whip, that one. He mentioned your episodes. Buddy, I can't blame you one bit with what your old man put you through. What he did to your family. I can't imagine such an ordeal. And what you saw in Germany, Lord Almighty. Young said he was real concerned about you, and he sounded about as genuine as a man could be. He also told me about your time at the psych ward at Walter Reed after the war."

Charlie looked Danaver directly in the eyes.

"I didn't kill her, Sheriff. And I'm not my father."

"The way you're tellin' me, well, I'm inclined to believe you."

"Thank you."

"It's just hard to accept. And they say an apple don't fall far from the tree."

"Are we done, Sheriff?"

"Not quite. If we go up to them caves, reckon you can help us find the body? We can bring the county chaplain if it'd make you feel better."

"I'm not going back up there. No way."

"You'd have full police protection."

"No. Besides, Cal told me not to trust you."

"She said that?"

"Yes, sir."

Danaver put a hand on Charlie's shoulder.

"Son, let me tell you. This whole thing is changin' shape now. We're movin' from a missin' persons case to a homicide investigation based on what you been tellin' me. That puts you in a precarious situation. You see that, don't you? If you can't help us find these villagers or moonshiners or whatever it is you said earlier, then you're goin' to be in what we call legal jeopardy. Now, when you told me what happened, you didn't seem to be lyin'. It sounded wild as all hell, and I don't know what to make of it. But your eyes weren't lyin'. So why don't you just help me? And for God's sake help your damn self."

"Doesn't sound like I got a choice in the matter."

"You always got choices. But you best believe me— they ain't always this straightforward." Danaver opened the door and there was a deputy sitting in the hall by Charlie's room. "Oh, one more thing. What did you eat while you were up there?"

"Eat?"

"Yes, eat. Jesus, Charlie. Why does everythin' have to be so damn hard? It's a simple question, ain't it? What did you chew and swallow to sustain your vitality durin' your absence?"

"Just what they served at the harvest festival."

"Just the one meal?"

"That's right. Cornbread and ribs. Some kind of potato fritters."

"Well you should be damn near skin and bones if that's all you ate."

"I can't explain it, Sheriff. I swear it was only a day."

"You know how crazy that sounds?"

Charlie folded his arms.

"I know."

"It's just that sometime when people get trapped to-gether, well—"

"Don't you even think that. I ain't a goddamn can-nibal."

"Okay. It's my job to ask questions, is all. It's got me in a quandary. The way I see it, it's a quandary we're both in so maybe we can help each other through it, Lord willin'."

It was snowing when they reached the village. Ici-cles hung from the eaves of the old wooden shacks and there was a light dusting of frost over the field grass. Nobody was about. When they reached the great or-chard, Charlie grabbed a barren twig and snapped it off. He studied it closely and broke off another small branch. And another.

All the trees were dead.

"Somethin' wrong, son?" said Danaver. He was standing with his wool jacket and wide-brimmed hat, thumb resting on the butt of his .38 revolver. His breath steamed when he spoke. The two other deputies stood the same way, watching Charlie carefully. Their name patches read Posnik and Samuels. Posnik car-ried a camera with a flashbulb around his neck.

"The trees must have died when—"

"When what?"

Charlie shook his head.

They tottered through the snow, peering into the crooked huts as they passed.

Charlie stood in the doorway of Oswyn's shack. The books were gone. The hand-carved figurines, too. He picked at the broken sill where they'd spackled it with mud, all the flowers long disintegrated.

"We've searched everything already," said one of the deputies. "We're missin' some damn good football for this shit."

"Give Charlie the time he needs," said Danaver. "He's helpin' us."

Charlie ran his fingertips over the walls of the shack, looking for any clue he could find. He looked back over the village. Even the bronze church bell was missing.

"They're all gone," he said. "They must have taken everything with them."

"Like Beech said, this place ain't likely to be occupied all year round. The roads get bad. No electricity."

"Somebody knows where they went. People don't just disappear. Don't you all know your own county?"

"It's a big county, Charlie. Lots of folks like to stay under the radar."

"What about Gwilym? Ever heard of a man with that name?"

"Like Willem with a G?" Danaver tossed a glance at the other two deputies. "You fellas ever heard the name?"

A pair of shaking heads.

"There was a woman named Abigail at the festival," said Charlie. "She was pretty, blond hair. I think she was the one they intended to kill until Cal showed up."

"I got a cousin named Abigail," said Posnik. "But she ain't pretty."

"I got a cousin Abigail, too," said Samuels. "I bet mine's uglier than yours."

Danaver cleared his throat.

"That's enough, gentlemen."

They moved on, down where the path switchbacked along the cliff face. The snow was deeper here, and the hike slowed. When they came to the mouth of the cave, they threw each other surprised looks.

"None of you fellas ever knew this was down here, did you?" said Charlie.

Danaver thumbed his flashlight and poked his head in.

"Get your guns out, boys. This here's a bear cave."

"Believe me," said Charlie. "The thing I saw was much worse."

Danaver shined the flashlight into the great dome above them.

"What you saw was up there?"

A quick nod.

They moved deeper into the cave.

One of the deputies remained at the entrance. He was shaking his head.

"I can't go in there with you fellas," he said.

"You afraid of bears, Samuels?" said Danaver.

"Not any more than anybody else. It's like the Lord is tellin' me not to. It's my Baptist blood pullin' me back. Somethin' ain't right, Sheriff."

Danaver gave Charlie a look, then swept the dangling roots with his gun arm and painted the light all around. Bones lay in piles over the floor of the cave. Severed tendrils coiled and overlapping each other. An old torch blackened at the end. The air smelled faintly of decay.

"These look like animal bones," said Danaver. He scooted them around with his boot. "Weird they're all stacked this way. You have anythin' to do with this, Charlie?"

"It was the demon. It moved them around like pieces on a board."

"The demon, huh?"

"They called it the Chessman. You can see why."

"And this is where it killed the girl?"

"Yes sir. She was hanging directly above us. Everyone just stood around, watching."

"And you stood watchin', too?" said Danaver.

"I tried to stop it, but I was too late. I think they drugged me and that's why I couldn't get to her in time."

Posnik called out to the sheriff.

"Over here. I think I found her."

Along the far wall of the cave lay a body covered in stones and roots. Insect skittered around their boots as they neared. They moved the stones one by one until a dead woman lay before them in a tattered, bloodstained dress.

"Lord in heaven," said Posnik, sweeping the hair off her face. "She's half-eaten. Ain't much left." He rose and snapped a photo and the cave blinked white.

"Goddamn," said Danaver. "Is that the dress she was wearin', Charlie?"

Charlie sat with his face buried in his hands. He looked up briefly and shut his eyes. The flesh was mostly gone, eyes missing. Lips and nose eaten away. Mouth jammed full of leaves. Decomposition had discolored the ground beneath her. The blond hair still looked soft and fine, like a wig on an old mummy.

"It's her," said Charlie.

Another bright flash. Shadows hammered across the cavewalls.

"You know for sure?"

"She had tattoos. You could check."

"Where? There's not much flesh."

"The insides of her thighs. Two moth tattoos."

Danaver nodded to the deputy, but the deputy shook his head.

"Can't it wait till we get back?" said Posnik. "Looks like a job for Doctor Jenson."

"I want to know."

Posnik checked with one hand covering his mouth and returned with a quick shake of his head. It looked like he was about to be sick.

"I jus' can't rightly tell, Sheriff. She's all et up."

They carried the remains across the empty village in a long canvas bag with hardly a word spoken between them. The snow picked up, building on the brims of their hats. After they secured the body in the covered truck bed, Danaver put a hand on Charlie's shoulder. He had a grim look, eyebrows furrowed in the way someone gives bad news. A pair of handcuffs rested in his hands.

"I want you to turn around, son."

"Wait. I didn't do this, Sheriff. I tried to stop it."

"I know you believe that."

"Because it's the truth. What does your gut say? Be honest, now."

Danaver straightened and blinked into the sky.

"Well. My gut says it's a matter for the courts. 'Course the DA will have his say as well. For now, this is just a psychiatric hold, Charlie. We'll make sense of it all somehow."

"Psychiatric hold? It happened like I said it did. What happened was crazy, I know. But I'm not crazy—the situation is crazy. Those people were crazy. You get that? I can't end up in some psych ward staring out the goddamn window all day, Sheriff. Don't you dare do that to me."

"Listen carefully. We had a witness at the liquor store down in Fig. This is the first time you're hearin' of it, but I wanted to get your reaction before takin' you in. She said you and Cal were havin' a spat in the parkin' lot before y'all disappeared. This would be on October the seventh if I'm not mistaken. Any of that true Charlie?"

"Well, it's true. Yes. But it was just a small disagreement."

"In hindsight it looks like a big deal, don't it?"

"It was nothing. I'd never hurt her—or anybody else."

"I want to believe you. I wish you'd told me a gang of moonshiners ran you off the road and you both got stranded up here. That would have been easier. But with all this magical demon business—it just has to be this way right now."

"It doesn't have to be any way. I did everything you asked."

"That'll probably help you some. How much it'll help will be up to the judge. Not me, you hear? The judge. Now turn around, dammit. I don't want to get physical."

Danaver fixed the cuffs over Charlie's wrists and instructed the others to put him in the backseat of the cruiser.

"You boys go ahead down the mountain 'fore the snow gets deep. I'll be right behind you."

"You'll be all right, Sheriff?" said Samuels.

"I'll be all right. I like to reflect whenever I see an incongruity such as this."

"A what, now?"

"Look around you, Samuels. It's so damn beautiful out here it could make a man cry. You could spend your whole life with a paintbrush in your hand and never capture this here landscape adequately enough. I dare you to try. And right through the middle of it comes a half-eaten ugly ol' corpse that used to be somebody. Reckon there's a lesson in it. Maybe it's so simple a lesson that it's confoundin' at the same time. Some lessons are like that. Maybe the lesson is there ain't no lesson to be had at all. I just don't rightly know yet."

"Well, I'd like to hear once you get a bead on it, Sheriff."

"I let you know, Samuels."

Danaver watched as they trundled down the rut road and across the meadow until they disappeared around the bend. He stood looking over the High Country hills and gullies, the landscape growing white and hazy at the edges. He took a long drink from a flask then he unbuttoned and relieved himself in the snow. As the steam rose, he noticed something half-buried just a few feet from the tips of his boots. A piece of cloth with red stitching. He shook off and buttoned his fly, toed at the buried object. When he gave it a kick, it jingled back at him. Danaver pulled it up and held it at a distance as if holding a dead rat by the tail.

"Goddamn," he said.

He flicked at the little bells running up the jumper.

The candlewick face, charred and scowling.

He dropped it and spat.

"Ain't that some wicked shit."

On the first day of spring, Charlie woke to the smell of apple pie. Sunlight brightened the windows and outside he could see an enormous willow tree gently swaying. He couldn't tell if it was morning or afternoon. He thought maybe the light looked too harsh to be morning. He closed his eyes and watched shapes tumbling red behind his eyelids. When he opened them again, Nurse Janet was wheeling him out of his room and down the hall. The aroma of pie lingered. It was somewhere near, tantalizingly so, but he couldn't see it. Maybe she was hiding it behind her back. The wheelchair glided gently down a ramp, spun on the landing, and went down another ramp. Sunshine warmed his face. He was in a large backyard with a freshly mowed lawn and hedges two stories high. A small fruit orchard stood to his right. Pink blossoms on their way out, dark green leaves taking their place.

"Isn't it a beautiful day, Charlie?" said Janet.

Charlie agreed with a slow nod.

"Pie," he said.

"Well don't you just have a one-track mind? I've got your pie, Mister. Don't you worry." She fitted a tray onto his lap and placed a bowl before him with a glistening mound of slop inside. "You want me to feed you, or do you want to try yourself?"

"Try," said Charlie.

"Well, all right, big boy."

She put a spoon in his hand and he recoiled with a groan.

"Oh, I'm sorry, fella." She rolled up the sleeves of his gown and inspected the dark bruises that covered his forearm, slightly yellowed at the edges. There were fresh scabs in the crook of his elbow where the injections had gone in haphazardly. "You really gave those orderlies a run for their money, Charlie. Everyone's talking about what a tough guy you are. Sorry they were so rough. But don't you worry—you'll get used to this place. Everyone gets used to it eventually. Besides, you get to spend time with me, don't you? You like me, right? It's not so bad with your pal Janet around."

He scraped at the pie-like substance and raised it to his lips.

Janet lit a cigarette, tousled his hair, and walked away. The wind picked up and a curtain of blossoms fanned out across the yard. Little pink and white petals like ticker tape. The fruit trees swayed. He saw children peeking out from behind the trunks. Mischievous gnome-like faces, growling and snarling. Charlie regarded them with an amused slant on his lips. They gathered the blossoms and poured them over their heads and fell to the ground writhing like worms on a wet sidewalk. They jumped up again and hopped in circles around his wheelchair, snapping their teeth and clawing the air.

The wind died just as suddenly as it came.

One by one, they disappeared into the orchard.

He listened for the song.

The chorus was very loud today, maybe hundreds of them.

Maybe thousands.

Charlie ate his pie, and it was very sweet.

EPILOGUE

In a pitch-black room, a bright square blinks onto a projector screen. A gang of bureaucrats sits around a conference table, arms folded. Against the pure white light, they look like typeface hammered onto a sheet of blank paper. Smoke eddies through a projector beam. Little red flares of tobacco cherries wink in the dark. Metal spools click over a reel mount.

A woman stifles a cry.

"You can leave when it starts, Barb."

A sniffle.

"No. I want to stay."

The projector rattles. The gears catch and the machine begins to purr.

Images form on the screen.

Apple trees at peak harvest. Dark fruit hangs low on the branches. A woman with a birdskull necklace lifts her arms to the sky in an operatic gesture and sings silently. You can almost hear it. Children gather in the freshly cut grass. They throw bizarre tantrums as if stung by a swarm of wasps, then go scurrying into the orchard. The scene cuts. A large bonfire, now. The brightness washes out the screen until a hand appears in the frame and adjusts the aperture. There are dancers circling the fire dressed in handmade clothes. Tunics and wool breeches and lace overdresses. They hold hands and spin around and around with laughing faces.

But the camera only wants one dancer.

She's blond and pretty and she's looking directly into the camera.

She laughs, says something to the man behind the lens.

The camera is very close now.

You can read her lips.

Come on, Charlie. Dance with me.

THE END

A NOTE ON THE TYPE

The text of this book is set in SchoolBook, a serif typeface designed by Elena Tzaregorodtseva at the Polygraphmash type design bureau in 1949-61. It is based on Shkolnaya ('School') typeface from 1939, a version of Century Schoolbook of American Type Founders, 1915-1923 by Morris F. Benton.

The digital version and condensed styles were designed for ParaType in 2005 by Manvel Shmavonyan.

Paratype has been designing, developing and distributing digital fonts since the 1980's. Their ever-growing library of hundreds of typefaces includes some of the most widely used fonts, such as PT Sans/Serif, Futura PT, DIN 2014, and Circe.

Composed by Clever Crow Consulting and Design,
Pittsburgh, Pennsylvania

ABOUT THE AUTHOR

C.W. Blackwell is an award-winning author and poet from the Central Coast of California. He has been a gas station attendant, a rock musician, and a crime analyst. He is a 2021 Derringer Award winner.

NOSETOUCH PRESS

Nosetouch Press is an independent book publisher
tandemly based in Chicago and Pittsburgh.
We are dedicated to bringing some of today's most
energizing fiction to readers around the world.

Our commitment to classic book design in a digital
environment brings an innovative and authentic
approach to the traditions of literary excellence.

*We're Out There
NOSETOUCHPRESS.COM
Horror | Science Fiction | Fantasy | Mystery
Supernatural | Folk Horror | Occult | Gothic | Weird